A KISS FOR A DEAD FILM STAR & OTHER STORIES

A KISS FOR A DEAD FILM STAR & OTHER STORIES

KAREN M. VAUGHN

BRAIN MILL PRESS  GREEN BAY, WISCONSIN

Published in the United States by Brain Mill Press.
STANDARD PRINT ISBN 978-1-942083-38-2
EPUB ISBN 978-1-942083-41-2
MOBI ISBN 978-1-942083-40-5
PDF ISBN 978-1-942083-39-9

Cover illustration © Samantha Battersby.
Cover design by Ranita Haanen.
Interior illustrations by Ann O'Connell.
Interior design by Williams Writing, Editing & Design.

Interested in reading more from Brain Mill Press?
Join our mailing list at www.brainmillpress.com.

CONTENTS

A Kiss
for a dead
Film Star

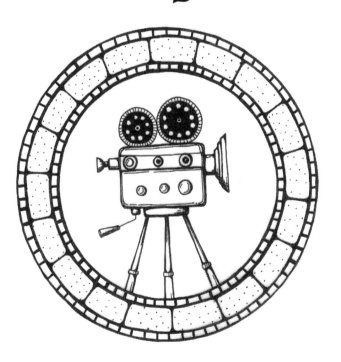

THE MOST BEAUTIFUL MAN IN THE WORLD HAS
DIED.

Sixteen-year-old Isaac Rubinstein sits on his cast-iron bed, in the tiny room he shares with his brother, and prepares to slit his wrists. Around him there is only melancholy, which has taken the form of various objects. It is masquerading as a sheet that has been fastened to a drawstring in the doorway. It has permeated the ink of a lithograph depicting the Old Opera House in Frankfurt. It has poured its essence into the wick of the oil lamp, into the small pine bureau, into the Bavarian lace curtains, into the plumes and flourishes of the green damask wallpaper. It has settled, also, over the tattered quilt, which has itself been buried beneath a doleful sea of photographs. These images are of particular relevance to Isaac's present state of despair. The settings and costumes they portray are multifold, but they all feature the same impossibly attractive man, gesticulating, or dancing, or just standing still. In this one, the man has been photographed wearing a sheik's flowing headdress. In that one, he holds a cigarette and exhales a sinuous column of smoke. In this one, he wears a powdered wig and a silk brocade coat, and in that one, he strums a Spanish guitar. And of course, here is the treasure at the root of Isaac's collection, a portrait of the man as he is emerging from the water, magnificently shirtless, with a small racing boat hoisted above his head.

The man in the photographs is Rodolfo Alfonso Raffaello Piero Filiberto Guglielmi di Valentina d'Antonguolla. He is Rudolph Valentino. The Great Lover. The most beautiful man in the world.

Isaac's own features are rather less impressive. He is tall but gangly, with a narrow chest that is little more than a monolithic slab. He has got the standard allotment of muscles, but you'd never know it to look at him. No matter how many games of stickball he plays, they remain just below the skin's surface, dreaming and undisturbed. (This is in stark contrast to his buddy Asher, who seems to have been born with calves like coconuts and biceps the size of summer peaches.)

Isaac's face is equally unexceptional. His eyes are set a bit close together, his lips are too thin, and his ears are pointed where they should be curved. These characteristics, combined with his unruly black hair and the overall gauntness of his physique, succeed in giving him the appearance of a half-starved animal. His habit of reading in public only serves to heighten this impression. Sometimes, when he is sitting alone on the tenement stoop, women will rise up from the pavement and bring him sandwiches.

But today there will be no sandwiches, and no stickball. The possibility for those things ended several hours earlier in a crowded hospital across town, when a glorious heart stopped beating, when a pair of lungs fluttered like moth's wings and then lay still, when a brain emptied out its last unknowable thoughts, when a doctor made a grave pronouncement to the assembled masses and watched the effect of his words slide outward like waves, provoking bouts of fainting and hysteria.

Isaac has been left with a single clear path. He must forge a connection with this man in the only way possible, and he must do so without delay. Already, he knows, the actor's body is beginning to divest itself of tiny particles of matter, which are lifting like delicate insects into the air around him. Already, the viscera are growing cold.

And so the razor blade makes its approach, sweeping downward onto a strip of blemish-free skin (one of the few qualities of which Isaac is unashamed).

He does it.

He doesn't do it.

His heart splits in two beneath a blue-enameled sky.

IN ONE PLACE, HIS BUBBE'S VOICE DISTURBS HIS REVerie before he can go through with it. She has woken up early from her postprandial nap. "Isaac, *luftmensch*," she pleads, "would you bring me a glass of water? I can feel my skin going scaly from the dryness."

For a moment Isaac is torn. It will be hours before anyone else comes home. Little Nate is still studying at the yeshiva, making the family ever so proud, and his mother will not be home from the garment factory until sundown, if not later. He has already considered that his bubbe will be left alone with his corpse for a good portion of the afternoon—a regrettable necessity —even as his blood is ebbing out and saturating the bar mitzvah quilt she made for him. But to leave her thirsty as well? Somehow it seems a needless cruelty. In the end he decides that the Deed will just have to wait until a more opportune moment.

"Coming, Bubbe," he answers at last. He slips the blade beneath his mattress and goes to help her, allowing the upended photographs to swirl behind him like a gust of papery leaves.

In the other place, where his bubbe continues her sleep uninterrupted, there is no such reprieve. Instead there is a tentative first cut, followed by several more that go much deeper. There is a gushing artery and the unforeseen pain of exsanguination. There is panic, regret, delirium. There is an attempt to arrange himself squarely on the bed so that his mother will not have too much of a mess to clean up. There is a sudden, amplified awareness of color—the color red, naturally, but also the color green as represented in the fronds of the damask, and beyond that, where the wallpaper curls out from the corner, a sea of blue-green that has stained the plaster for decades, eschewing all the family's efforts to paper over its wildness. There is the memory of being two years old, walking with his mother and father on the beach, swinging like a bell between them. There is a descending fog and, from a distance, the high keening wail of a grief-stricken bubbe. And when it is all over, there is a presence that crawls from the wreckage of a ruined shell, propelling itself through a long and shadowy tunnel, struggling, gasping, swimming hard against the membranous current on its way to some unfathomable goal.

Isaac's father, a former shipyard worker, was killed in the Great War when Isaac was only seven years old. This left his mother to become the primary breadwinner of the family. For fifteen years now she has worked six days a week at the Kops Bros. clothing building. Before that, though, she was an employee at the infamous Triangle Shirtwaist Factory, and it was there that she witnessed the most destructive fire on record. Isaac had only heard her speak of it once.

She told the story on a late December evening, and she and their neighbor Mrs. Abelsdorff were sitting at the kitchen table with their hands cupped tightly around bowls of hot cabbage soup. Both women were redolent of sweat and tailor's chalk, so that without any effort Isaac was able to close his eyes and imagine himself in the factory as the events unfolded, among the endless oak tables where the seamstresses were lined up in rows like sweet corn.

She had known it would happen, she said. She had known because the fabric scraps were collecting in drifts on the factory floor and the tissue paper patterns that had been hung above the tables were beginning to whisper like wraiths. Moreover, a rising tide of shirt-waists was foaming up around their ankles. Sewing machines hunkered like frightened animals. Even the bolts of cotton that snaked through the room carried warnings in their ragged edges. Auspices were everywhere. But what could she do? She'd have been fired if she left her station, and there was a baby at home to think about. Over and over her gaze returned to Til-lie, the black-haired woman across the table, and as it did she allowed herself to be reassured by her friend's tireless fingers, her unassailable calm. She ignored the stone of dread that was taking shape at the pit of her stomach.

(What if she had left then? Isaac wondered. Would it have been better for her? To have only heard about the catastrophe hours later? To have sat in Ratner's and sighed like tree boughs in autumn and murmured 'oy-oy-oy' with her fellow survivors? Would she be a different person if she had not seen the bones of her sisters turned to pulp and ash?)

As closing time approached, things began to go wrong. From the ceiling there came a dull and droning noise, and at first Isaac's mother believed it to be nothing more than the creaking of pipes several stories up. But the noise grew louder by the second, and more clamorous, until it sounded as if a massive thunderstorm were bearing down on the building. Someone cried out. Someone spoke the word 'fire.' Someone abandoned her treadle and flung herself like a captured bird through the open door. Bit by bit, the tragedy was blooming into the fullness of its being.

Already, a dense canopy of smoke had formed overhead. It seemed to have come out of nowhere, and it was roiling, churning, stealing air and visibility from those who had not yet decamped the factory floor. Panic took hold. The women pushed past one another. They elbowed. They shoved. They poured themselves down the staircase like water. Their screams coalesced into a single blistering howl, a keening siren-sound that played havoc with the ears and caused many of the fleeing workers to lose their equilibrium, tumbling headfirst onto the mass of flesh below.

His mother's part in this exodus did not take long—she had been stationed on the third floor. Those inhabiting the upper floors, however, were not so lucky. Some inhaled lethal amounts of smoke or became trapped beneath overturned equipment. A few were trampled like clover. Many, far too many of them, jumped.

Once outside, Isaac's mother had stared, mesmerized, as the solid stone exterior transformed into a vertiginous wall of flame, occasionally darkened by the shape of a falling body. Several times she had stooped to vomit. Josie did not come out. Abigail did not come out. Nor did Alva, Razi, Ester, Lea, Hannah, Milly, or Elizaveta. Naomi and Pazia were among those who had jumped from the ninth floor. In their absence was a mounting swell of grief. Already the women wore it like a perfume; it permeated their hair and issued in clouds from their pores. Even Tillie was changed. She was stoic as always, but her eyes seemed to have become a pair of blackened pits, dead stars orbiting in a binary system. "It's a *shanda*," she said simply.

The Triangle Shirtwaist Fire was his mother's Great War, and it seemed to take something essential out of her. Once vibrant and sunny of a disposition, she now glides through life in near silence, a mere specter in the halls.

There are times when he can barely see her. She will appear in the doorway after work, and for a moment he will have a vivid glimpse of her cupid's face, of cheeks that are petal pink from the cold, of short, wavy hair peeking out from beneath the brim of her felt hat, before the features begin to fade again and the already slight frame wisps away into the spaces between the furniture. She is tired, he knows that. The stain of mourning has never left her. The last time he saw her express any happiness at all was at a Shabbat-eve meal three months earlier, when Little Nate, who was really only two years his junior, announced his plans to become a rabbi. She leapt up from the table, knocking over her glass in the process, and enveloped the bespectacled boy in a ferocious and lingering embrace. Isaac just sat there and closed his eyes against the scene. He was pretending that Valentino was sitting beside him, holding the kiddush cup.

His bubbe has started to nod off again in her chair. A copy of *Der Tog* lies open across her lap, along with the obligatory magnifying glass for reading the small print of the obituaries. Isaac thinks about proceeding with his plan. But by now the lamp in the bedroom has begun to flicker weirdly, even though he refilled the oil not half an hour ago, and so he departs from the tenement earlier than necessary and makes his way to the theater where he works.

Crossing Orchard Street, he plots his next attempt. His only regret is that he won't be the first to carry out this ultimate declaration of loyalty. God knows how many women the world over have already collapsed under the weight of their anguish. So far he is aware of several who attempted suicide outside the Polyclinic Hospital and several more who succeeded in their own homes. And there are stories of hundreds more. Even now they are doing it. They are taking poison. They are drowning themselves in the East River. They are placing their heads in ovens and turning on the gas. They are flinging themselves in front of automobiles and wrapping their necks in challah-style nooses. They are holding pocket pistols in their mouths and pulling the trigger. And they are jumping. Of course they are jumping. If reports are to be believed, there was a woman early this morning who ascended the Gothic carapace of the Woolworth Building in her best Sunday dress and leapt from somewhere near the top. (*Why is this such a recurring theme in New York?* Isaac wonders.) A lipsticked copy of one of Valentino's poems was said to have been found folded up inside her brassiere. Furthermore, the city's infrastructure seems to be carrying out its own mechanistic form of bereavement. Water lines have been bursting, suddenly and without provocation, as if this newly plumbed circulatory system, this lifeblood that pulses beneath the streets, has itself yielded to despair and laid open its veins to the sweltering August heat. Construction of the Holland Tunnel has likewise ground to a halt, as the underwater caisson where the iron rings are bolted together unaccountably lost pressure and had to be evacuated. Bank clocks have ceased their functioning. Store awnings have come loose from the walls and lowered themselves to half-mast. It feels like the world is ending, or at least one particular version of it.

At the theater everyone is talking about what has happened. An old man shakes his head at his wife. "He was a rare thing," he says. "No way Hollywood'll let another immigrant into its ranks. Mark my words, there'll be nothing but lily-whites from here on out."

Beside him a trio of middle-aged women trade stories about their first experience watching a Valentino movie. One of them laughs conspiratorially: "I was on fire for weeks. My husband thought he'd died and gone to heaven." Behind this group two men in suit jackets are chattering about the possibility of a public funeral. And over by the wall there is a girl of about fifteen who has collapsed against an old poster of *Blood and Sand*. She is weeping openly, and it isn't long before a group of boys begins to mock her.

"He was a fop," one of them says loudly, tilting his head in her direction.

"Choked on his own pomade," laughs another. "This ulcer business is just a cover story."

But the girl doesn't seem to hear them. She continues with her lamentations, sobbing her heart out at some solitary grotto of the mind where nothing exists but herself and the man on the poster, where the insults of others are no more than gnats to be swatted away. Isaac wishes he could be so brave.

"I heard he had love notes from *men* in his pockets when he was taken to the hospital," a third one offers.

"Always knew he was a three-letter man."

They all laugh.

"Well," says the first boy, turning his attention back to his friends. "He was definitely wearing ladies' under-things when they brought him in. It's true! No one could believe it, but there they were, plain as day. Red lace knickers and fancy garters. The doctors swore everyone to secrecy."

The conversation then veers off into the direction of the lewd, and Isaac, while inflamed by their remarks about his hero, decides to ignore them and get started with his nightly duties.

Asher greets him as he steps into the projection room. The young man is breathless, his green eyes bright with excitement. "Can you believe this?" he exclaims. "It's like he was President of the United States or something! I know, I know . . . you're a fan. But dingus. Even *you've* got to admit some people are overreacting."

Isaac is suddenly embarrassed. "Well I don't know," he begins uncertainly. "Sometimes people have different ideas about what's important."

"You got that right," Asher laughs. "I caught my ma crying at the ticket booth earlier today. My own ma! I ask her what's so terrible and she says she's thinking of Aunt Hedya back in Leipzig. Fat chance. More like she's gone weak for the Sheik."

Isaac's friendship with Asher began eight years earlier, a few weeks after his best mate, Hymie, died of influenza. Asher had just lost his own close friend to the same illness, and thus it was only natural that the two boys would forge a wholeness out of their separate halves. It happened after a marathon game of stickball. Asher asked him over for dinner, and Isaac, flattered by this invitation from an older, more popular boy, eagerly accepted.

Asher's family has run the neighborhood theater for upwards of twelve years. When Isaac was ten, Asher was able to secure him a much-coveted job as a gofer for the establishment. His duties included assisting the projectionist (who was too busy hand cranking the film to do anything else), changing reels when necessary, fetching coffee for the organist, and delivering the hourly ticket counts to the manager, Asher's father. Contrary to his initial hopes, Isaac found that he was far too busy running errands to watch any of the movies during work hours.

He *was*, however, able to glimpse them in a piecemeal fashion—a dramatic segment here, a passionate embrace there, and of course the occasional frame of calligraphied dialogue, which was like a page torn from some medieval text. Little by little these fragments began to drift together in his brain, converging like continents, until he was left with a memory of having seen each film in its entirety.

In this way he became familiar with the work of Charlie Chaplin and Edna Purviance. Douglas Fairbanks and Mary Pickford. He loved the excitement of the audience in those first few moments when the lamps dimmed and the images flared into being on the screen. He loved the heft of the reels, which were like the prodigious wheels of some ancient chariot. Most of all he loved the sense of captured time, the sense that all things ephemeral could be preserved indefinitely with the aid of this elegant new medium. Death itself might come, but the actors would be ever youthful, ever vibrant on the screens, their high cheekbones and luminous skin enshrined for eternity.

Asher's younger sister, Doralee, sometimes followed Isaac around as he performed his duties, her little black patent shoes leaving galactic whorls in the dust on the floor of the projection room. Doralee was every bit as enthralled by the movies as he was, if not more so, and Isaac had a wonderful time entertaining her with the farcical voices he created for each of the actors. The voice of the villain was typically a gravelly snarl, while the heroine was rendered with a squeaky falsetto that always sent the girl into helpless peals of laughter. Sidekicks delivered their lines with a southern drawl. Ministers and other religious persons often sounded as if they had had too much to drink. Only the hero spoke clear and pure as a bell. Try as he might, Isaac could not bring himself to treat this character type with anything but the utmost earnestness.

The longer Isaac worked there, the more his life began to take on a kind of duality. During the day, he steeled himself against the various constrictions of the tenement: the overachieving brother; the distant mother; the school assignments that did nothing but demonstrate to the world how unexceptional he was; even the green paint that kept appearing beneath his fingernails, as if he had been clawing at the walls in his sleep. But in the evenings—oh yes, in the evenings, everything was different. There was glamor. There was mystery. There was divine justice. It was only in this rarefied atmosphere that Isaac felt he could truly breathe, within this strange golden existence that was like a sliver out of someone else's life.

And then, in his eleventh year, the reels arrived for a film called *The Four Horsemen of the Apocalypse*. As Isaac watched this new leading man tango across the screen in a Spanish hat and gaucho pants—eyes darkly seductive, limbs sinuous as a panther's—he felt the gears within himself quietly shifting into place. He knew he was falling in love.

"Will you boys shut up?" hisses the projectionist, bringing Isaac back to the present. "I got a show in two minutes and I haven't finished looking over the chart."

Asher dismisses this with a wave of his hand. "The folks down there don't know how fast it's supposed to be cranked. Why don't you just make it up as you go along? No one'll know any different."

"I'd know," the projectionist responds huffily, shifting his rather large posterior on the metal stool beneath him. "There's a right and a wrong way to do everything, young man. And anyway, suppose I go too fast through an action bit and nobody can tell what's going on? What then?"

"Well then I guess you should get canned," Asher laughs, and hurriedly steps out the door before the older man can take a swing at him. In the hallway he turns back to Isaac with a grin. "Pa's trying to get the reels to *Cobra* so the theater can have some kind of memorial for him. I'd prefer *The Son of the Sheik*, myself. It's funnier and there's more sexy stuff. But Pa says that one won't sell as many tickets. Which one do you think we should get?"

"*Horsemen* is the first one I saw, so I'd have to vote for that."

"Eh, that one's okay, I guess. At least it's got a war to keep things interesting."

"And a ghost."

"And a ghost! I forgot!" he exclaimed. "How great would that be? To be visited by a ghost, I mean. A couple summers ago my cousin Reuben was going on and on about how he'd seen the ghost of a little girl hovering at the foot of his bed. Said she was wearing a long white shawl and one of those giant hoop skirts like they had back in Lincoln's day. Knowing Reuben, though, he was just trying to get attention. You got to ask yourself: why would a spirit bother showing itself to him, of all people? He's a knucklehead. Might as well show itself to a fire hydrant for all the good it'd do."

Isaac laughs appreciatively. Just then a voice booms out from the projection room. "Rubinstein! I need another marking pencil in here."

"All right, Morty. I'll have it for you in a few." And off he goes, leaving Asher to wander about the theater.

Later on, when the six o'clock showing has started, Isaac goes to get the ticket count from Asher's mother. But when she opens her mouth to speak, all he can hear is a peculiar crackling noise where her voice should be.

He is taken aback. What is going on? He can see the woman smiling at him, with her flawless skin and the cherry-red lipstick that drives the neighborhood boys wild with lust, and he can tell by her expression that as far as she is concerned, nothing is amiss. She speaks to him again. This time he watches her lips move, but it makes no difference. His ears are filled with the same crackling sound as before, a strange ethereal sound that is somehow reminiscent of the snaps and sparks of a great bonfire. Looking around, he cannot fathom the source of the interference. Could it have something to do with the lights on the marquee? He doesn't think so. He's heard them sizzle in the rain, and the effect was more like the buzzing of a small bee. What else then? He finds himself seized by an unaccountable sense of dread. What is happening? Has he lost his mind?

Asher's mother is still peering at him expectantly, and he realizes he needs to explain himself. "I'm sorry, Mrs. Grünbaum," he says finally. "I'm not feeling too good. My ears are ringing, and I can't hear what you're saying. Would you please write it down for me?"

She complies, but not before giving his arm a gentle squeeze. It is such a tender gesture that he nearly breaks down in tears right then.

Back inside, Isaac has to duck into a supply closet so as not to fall apart in front of the patrons. The despair that was kept at bay during his conversation with Asher has now come back with a vengeance, and all he can do is sink to the floor and give himself over to it. He begins to weep uncontrollably. The world, he decides, is too full of horrors. The incident with Asher's mother is proof enough of that. And yet here he is, fetching pencils and relaying ticket counts instead of accomplishing his objective. What is wrong with him? Has he, like Hamlet, fallen into doubt after postponing a necessary action? He finds he is even having second thoughts about his chosen method. Slitting his wrists, after all, would be a personal act, when what he really wants is to declare his feelings before the entire city in a way that is commensurate with his devotion. He thinks of the other devotees and considers his options.

Guns are impractical; he has never even held one. The stove or noose approach would have to be planned in advance. Drowning would be easier, but his terror of water makes the idea unappealing. All at once, like a death's-head moth alighting on his brow, the correct course reveals itself to him. He will jump. Like so many New Yorkers before him, he will simply locate a tall building and leap from its highest point. It's the perfect method. It has the advantage of being over with quickly, and there is a symbolic resonance to it, which will place him among the ranks of the city's indelible dead. As a bonus, it is a method that requires no preparation.

Yes, he says to himself. *That woman at the Woolworth Building had it exactly right. That's what I shall do. Except instead of a skyscraper, I'll do it from the top of this theater, because that's where I first fell in love.* Having decided this, he feels suddenly calm. He proceeds to the kitchenette, where he prepares a hot mug of coffee for the organist, mixing in a bit of the homemade whiskey that Mr. Grünbaum keeps in the cabinet for special occasions.

FROM THE BEGINNING THERE WAS SOMETHING SPEcial about the man. His features were delicately exotic. He had a prominent Roman nose, jet-black brows, and sensuous lips, which combined in such a way as to give him an air of insouciant mischief. Sometimes Isaac would stay late at the theater so that he could examine the man's tiny form on the individual frames of film. It was astonishing to him that something so small could, with the mere application of light and a magnifying lens, produce such a sublime experience within the audience. And yet, shrunk down on a strip of celluloid, these images were his own secret treasure, just the right size that a boy might carry them around with him in his heart. He often caressed Valentino's likeness with gloved fingers, and he liked to imagine that wherever he was, the actor could sense this remote contact. Perhaps his cheeks burned from the touch. Perhaps, each time it happened, he stretched out his own thoughts to a hungry universe. Perhaps he, too, was desperate to be found.

Eventually, Isaac came to feel that these few minutes a day spent in adoration were not enough, and he began to clip photographs out of newspapers and fan magazines so that he could continue the ritual in the semiprivacy of his own home. He kept these bound in a folder, which he placed beneath his pillow, hoping the images would filter into his dreams. But as many such photos as he was able to amass, he found it was never enough to perfect the bond that was forming between the man and himself. Some crucial element was missing. And then, on an ice-encrusted day in February, he discovered what it was.

It began when he overheard some boys in Latin class singing the praises of a certain a tobacco store, just off of Pitt Street, where erotic portraits of famous actresses could be purchased. A light seemed to go off inside him. He took the trolley that very afternoon, and found the place just where the boys had said it was, down a some-what dingy side street, nestled between a shoe repair shop and a bakery specializing in blintzes. It took him several minutes to muster the courage to go in. Once inside, he again lost his nerve and began to meander around the perimeter of the shop. He wasn't sure how to proceed. He wished that he had at least considered what he was going to say and that he hadn't been so impulsive in making this trip. He was conscious, too, that a deep blush was rising in his cheeks. In order to conceal this, he kept leaning in toward the merchandise as if to examine the various tropical scenes depicted on the cigar box lids.

"Help you?" came the gruff voice of the shopkeeper after what seemed like hours.

By then there was no turning back. Isaac took a deep

breath and approached the counter, doing his best to affect an air of indifference. "Yes," he began. "I've heard you sell . . . special photos. What I want to know is, are they only of women?"

The shopkeeper was short, with a rather brawny build, and he had an anchor tattoo on his wrist that suggested a recent stint in the navy. He stared at Isaac without comprehension. "What are you, some kind of pervert?"

Isaac faltered. "What? No . . . they're for somebody else. She's shy . . . she didn't want to come in herself. Sent me to do the dirty work, you know."

The man's face brightened when he heard this, and he gave out a sudden, boisterous laugh. "Ha! I'm just joshing, kid. Lemme see if I've got something you want." He withdrew a large gray hatbox from beneath the cash register and spread out its contents on the counter. "This what your lady friend is after?" Isaac looked down and was at once lost in a vast sea of flesh. His consciousness began to drift. He rose and fell with the billowing muscles, bobbing among flotillas of chest hair and broad, glistening shoulders that seemed to have been rubbed down with oil. The radiance of the display stunned him. He felt sun-blinded by those glossy bodies, most of which were in a full state of anatomical exposure. The pictures were vulgar, and they were exhilarating. However, they weren't what he came for.

"No, no, no," Isaac protested, blushing again. "Don't you have any of famous actors? Like, say, Valentino?"

"Ah, I see! Only the best for this young lady, eh?" The man flashed him a lewd grin and produced a second, smaller box from beneath the counter. "These ain't dirty as such," he explained, leafing through the stack and setting the selected pictures in front of Isaac. "Just what you might call candid. They was taken by a private photographer from out west. Hardly anyone has seen them, though, so you'll understand if I ask a bit more. They're for . . . your big sister?"

"My mother."

"Ha!" the man guffawed, delighted with this answer. "Should have known. Sometimes I think these older dames got more going on 'tween their thighs than girls half their age. No offense, no offense!" he added hurriedly, seeing the flash of anger that crossed Isaac's face.

The price was steep, but in the end he paid it. These photographs provided a heretofore unseen glimpse into the actor's private life, and it was worth the month's salary that it cost him just to get his hands on a single one of them. It was even worth the humiliation that occurred at the conclusion of the transaction, when the shopkeeper observed the condition of his young customer's trousers and promptly booted him from the store.

That night, after Little Nate went to sleep, he carefully removed the photos from their wax bag and held them up to the amber light that was filtering in from the kitchen. He flipped through them until he found his favorite, which he had placed near the back in case his overprotective bubbe decided to conduct a search of his belongings upon his return home. Tenderly, he scrutinized the image. The waves in the background, the otherworldly lighting, the sinewy aspect of the man himself as he supported a two-man racing scull—Isaac committed all of these details to memory so that he might call them forth at some future date. His friends believed that Valentino was insufficiently masculine. What did they know? This was a man in the truest sense. This was a man who was lean, vital, athletic, buoyant in his stance, protean in his capabilities, with an appealing outline of muscles that rose like islands from his abdomen. It didn't hurt that he was wearing bathing shorts of the thinnest material—so thin, in fact, that Isaac had no trouble imagining what it would be like to press that smooth-textured fabric between his fingers (to say nothing of the emergent landscape beneath it). And of course there was his face—that irenic face—which was absurdly beautiful, as if it belonged not to a human but to some celestial being that had plunged to earth, setting the air aflame as he fell.

Pressing his thumbnail to the picture, Isaac traced the outline of a body. "I'm here," he said under his breath. "I love you."

THE CLOCK IN THE BANK TOWER NEXT DOOR RINGS eight o'clock. By now the shorts, newsreels, and serials have all been shown, and Pauline has once again been rescued from her most recent peril. Lionel Barrymore's *The Bells* is playing for the last time that night. Isaac sweeps up the spilled popcorn in the lobby. He climbs a ladder and changes the letters on the marquee. He empties the trash bins. And when the shimmering shapes begin to appear just outside his range of vision, he studiously ignores them. He is more tranquil than he has been in ages, having re-committed himself to his plan.

As the minutes flow on, however, he begins to regret that he has not said good-bye to those closest to him. To Asher and Doralee. To his bubbe, with her sunken eyes and her hair like copper wire. To the infallible Little Nate, who would one day be a rabbi. To kind Mrs. Grünbaum. And of course to his mother . . . his mother.

Somehow it had not occurred to him to consider her feelings in this matter. For so long there had been only animosity between them, a gradual accretion of resentments that grew over their hearts like hard coral. Now he finds he is able to sympathize with her again.

He thinks about her widowhood. He thinks about the fire that took more than thirty of her friends. He thinks about the lifetimes she has spent at the factory, and how every day for her is a reincarnation into the same bleak world. He even thinks about the silk-ribboned cloche that she wore with pride until he told her she looked like one of the Keystone Kops. (How could he have been so cruel? He had not even felt a pang of remorse afterward.) Indeed, her face contains a record of all these sufferings. The wrinkles branching out from her eyes and mouth are those of a woman ten years her senior. Weariness seems to have settled over her like a mask, and for the first time it occurs to him that his mother did the best she could while raising him. She worked herself ragged so that he could be a creature unfettered by need, so that he could be like the golden children of the city, the ones who laughed and shot marbles or played Ringolevio, who spent their money on cheap barrel pickles, who got in fist-fights over nothing, who burned through the streets like rogue comets, their bodies aching and resplendent with light. This was all she had wanted for her sons. Was it her fault Isaac was a different breed of *boychick*?

He ponders writing a note to explain himself. But when he thinks of what it would say, he realizes that he can't do the act justice. His motivations are too delicate, too pure, too like a cloud of paper sparrows to be rendered into the crudeness of language.

Eventually, the film comes to an end. The audience emerges from the deep-sea darkness of the theater and enters the luminous lobby, blinking at the brightness, filling their lungs instinctively like swimmers who have come to the surface after a long dive. Soon they are voicing their opinions about the film.

"Barrymore was spectacular," someone says. "So distinguished."

"The plot was shameful. Notice how it's always the Jew who goes and gets himself murdered?"

"How ridiculous to make a movie based on a poem."
"Edward Phillips is handsome, but he's no Rudy."
No he isn't, thinks Isaac. *Not by a long shot.*

WHEN ALL THE PATRONS HAVE GONE, HE SWEEPS UP the lobby a final time and waves good-night to Mr. and Mrs. Grünbaum, who are busy tallying the day's receipts in the back office. Asher is nowhere to be found. Where could he have gone? Could he have popped over to Ratner's for some coffee and mandelbread? Or could it be that he went out dancing with that rabbi's daughter from Anshe Slonim, the one he just bought that fancy cigarette case for, and neglected to tell Isaac his plans? Isaac feels an unexpected pang at this injustice. And yet, he can acknowledge that his friend's absence is probably for the best. Seeing Asher's fresh-scrubbed face right now, all ruddy and glowing with ebullient life, might keep him from doing what needs to be done.

With nothing further to keep him, Isaac makes his way to the back stairwell and begins his ascent. Eight stories is not all that high for a New York building, but it will be enough. Stride by stride he goes. Up, up, and always up. He moves slowly at first, then quickens the cadence of his feet until he is practically leaping from step to step. His limbs are throbbing from the exertion. His heart is a smoldering coal. Before long he begins to feel tiny shocks whenever he touches the banister, his fingertips prickling on the metal surface as if the whole length of it has been electrified. With every contact a million tiny messages are received into his skin. A million prayers, a million warnings, a million pleas for forbearance, each passing through the slender conduit of his body and leaving traces of itself behind. Their clamor rises in his ears, seemingly amplified by the resonance of the cement stairwell. Still, he endures. He races upward as if outrunning a flood. He fills his mind with the comforting imagery of his beloved, with soothing glimpses of slicked-back hair and volcanic eyes and cheekbones that are bright like harvest moons. He finds his sanctuary within this apparition of lineaments.

Despite their physical differences, Isaac has always believed that he and the movie star are kindred spirits, made of the same ethereal stuff and equally unclassifiable. So it is that the impulse to jump assumes a protective quality. He imagines throwing himself onto the flower-strewn casket, and he thinks, *Yes, I will cover you up with my broken body, so that for once you will be anonymous, so that you will finally be free from public scrutiny, so that you will no longer be afraid to love who you love.* The idea appeals to him, and he clings to it for solace. He flies up the stairs, faster and faster, pushing hard against the persistent drag of the banister, the agitated murmurs which are like anchors in his flesh, so that when he reaches the top he knows there will be nothing left but to go shooting like a bullet across the roof and into the silvered nets of infinity.

And now his hand is on the door, and he is saying good-bye to the city that has been his world.

Good-bye to the Central Park trees, to the public gardens with their botanical profusion in spring and their hibernations in winter, the husked carapaces of bulbs lying below ground like sleeping children, good-bye to ruby-stemmed vegetables at the market, to the redolent earth outside his building when it is stirred by April rains, to insects that seek out light and the warmth of newly drawn blood, good-bye to mechanical things as well, to the streamlined trains, to motorcars, to foundries and shipyards, to suspension bridges spun from steel loins, good-bye to the East River, laid like a silent trap against the land, good-bye to the boys who inhale hardship and exhale beauty, to the one boy who can wound like no other, good-bye to sorrows that are heavy slung and those that are fleeting, good-bye to the hothouse of memory (what will happen to his memories when he is dead? will they fall away like scales, like ashes scattered on a summer wind?), good-bye to the sea-green walls of home, to Shabbat candles, to the mezuzah clinging grasshopper-like to the door frame, to the sweetness of the spice box when passed from hand to hand, to his father's leather gloves and his mother's dusty viola, locked away in their separate cabinets, to *Der Tog* and the secrets of his bubbe's girlhood that he will never know, and to bookish Little Nate, who used to worship him, and who once bequeathed to him his prized cat's eye shooter—the one with the cream-and-gold ribbons inside—just because he asked for it.

Hello to his destiny. Hello to the end of his various sufferings. Hello to the incandescent figure in the matador's costume whose arms follow the curvature of planets. He, too, will streak across the sky, even if it means being no more than the dim afterglow that follows the shooting star.

The door swings open, creaking on its seldom-used hinges, and he thinks, *I am ready.*

AND SO HE RUSHES OUT ONTO TO THAT WINDSWEPT roof, full of fire and rapture and longing. But before he can take those last few steps into oblivion, something stops him. A phantasm in white appears beside him, and he is so startled that he lurches obliquely away from it, stumbling against a chimney and collapsing into an awkward heap just short of the ledge.

For a moment he doesn't look up—he is afraid of what he will find—but when he does he is relieved to see it is only Doralee standing there, laughing, dressed all in white. She helps him to his feet and takes note of the scrapes on his hands. "Did that happen just now? Bunny! I was just trying to scare you, not maul you."

"No . . . it's okay," he replies, still gasping for breath after his rapid climb. Then curiosity overtakes him and he finds himself peering over the edge at the thoroughfare below. It seems impossibly distant to him now. The cars move along like great rafts of seaweed, circumnavigating the dark shoals that divide the road into north- and south-facing tributaries. His gaze falls closer to the building, and he pinpoints the exact place where he would have landed had this latest attempt not been foiled. A clean rectangle of sidewalk, set between two ornate lampposts. Well-lit, like a movie screen. *I can still do it*, he thinks.

"Looked like you were about to jump just then," says Doralee with a smile. "Not that I'd blame you. Sometimes my brother tells jokes so bad I want to end it all, too."

Recovering himself somewhat, Isaac considers for the first time her changed appearance. He still thinks of Doralee as a child, but of course she's thirteen now. Her newly cropped hair floats to the side. She still wears black patent shoes, and yet her dress is that of a modern young woman—sleek and columnar, with a ruffled hem that only reaches her knees. She is good-looking, just like her mother.

He musters a small grin. "Are you kidding? I never get tired of hearing the one about the whore and the one-legged fisherman. That one's still fresh as a daisy."

Doralee makes a great show of being outraged. "Isaac Rubinstein! Well I never!" But she is still smiling. "Confidentially," she adds, leaning close, "I've been thinking about slitting my wrists all day, just like those gals I been reading about in the newspaper. It really is too sad what happened to him, isn't it? Ma said to me this morning, someone that gorgeous ought to have been taken up in a chariot like Elijah, instead of dying in a crummy hospital."

"So true," says Isaac.

"Kinda feels like the world is over without him. Like all the prettiness has been emptied out and there's only ugly, shabby things left."

Isaac nods emphatically. "That's exactly it! You do have a way of putting things."

"That's me!" she declares. "The poet of Orchard Street."

"That's you," he says with a wink, and here he decides to make a jest of the thing dearest to him. "You know, if you still want to pay tribute to the Latin Lover, we could always take a little walk off the ledge here. Right now. We could hold hands maybe, like we were just taking a dip in the pool. Or, if you prefer, I could let you go first."

"So gallant!" she laughs, and the way she crinkles up her nose amazes him, it is so much like Asher. "Look, this may sound daffy," she says after a moment. "But I thought I heard a voice telling me to come up here. Isn't that wild?"

A sudden wind sweeps across the rooftop. It catches the hem of Doralee's dress and causes it to billow outward, so that he cannot help but think of the *tachrichim* they wrapped his zayde in before they buried him, before the funeral, when the family got their last mortal glimpse of a man transformed by disease and old age and the shards of earthen pottery that made mosaics of his eyes, and whose countenance toward the end had taken on an unsettling lapidary quality, like the door of an abandoned hovel, even as his muscles hardened into so much ballast.

Isaac can feel gooseflesh now, forming along his neck and arms. "What kind of voice? What did it sound like?"

"Well, to be honest," she says, "it sounded like *you*. Daffy, right? It was like you were right beside me, whispering in my ear, which made me blush all over till I realized no one was there."

"Oh . . . I see."

"Look, I know it was my imagination, but it seemed so real to me. One of those waking dreams I guess. For a second I was sure it was a ghost. *Your* ghost. But how could it be your ghost when you're right here in front of me, not dead? See what I mean? I can be so stupid sometimes. Ma always says I got too much fancy in my noodle and not enough sense. So I tried to ignore it, but the voice didn't go away, and I figured as long as I was hearing you I might as well do what you said and see what happened. I mean, it's not like you were telling me to murder a family in their beds or something."

"So what *did* the voice say?"

"Well it just said you were in danger and I needed to find you. You weren't actually going to do something to hurt yourself, were you? Oh! I just had a thought.

Maybe it *was* your ghost, but from some other reality where you really did do away with yourself, and it came to stop you from doing the same thing here."

Isaac has to smile at the absurdity of this. "That sounds awfully complicated."

"Well who are we to judge what goes on in the spirit world? I'm sure they have their own communication system, like us with the telephone exchange. Probably not all that hard for them."

He shakes his head. "I had no idea you believed in this sort of stuff."

"I don't, really. Guess this heat is making me kind of screwy."

"Yeah? What was your excuse before?"

She punches him in the shoulder.

"Okay, okay," he says, laughing. "But there's one flaw in your charming theory. Why would the ghost have to use *you* as an intermediary? Couldn't he talk to me directly?"

"Hmm," she says, furrowing her brow. "Maybe that other version of you couldn't get through to this version, or maybe his voice just blended right in with your other thoughts, so he started talking to me instead cause he knew I'm a daffy girl with a crush and I'd listen. See, I've always been kind of sweet on you. Did you know that? Asher thinks we'll get hitched one day, but I'm guessing that's not in the cards."

Isaac is taken aback. "Oh . . . I see," he stammers. "I like you, Doralee. It's just that . . . well . . ."

But Doralee interrupts him before he can embarrass himself further. "I was kidding!" she cries. "Just kidding. Really. Don't think I'm such a sap, please. I couldn't bear you thinking that about me."

"Fine," he says, and in truth he is relieved not to have to answer. "I'll think whatever you want me to think. How about that?"

"Sounds good," she agrees. "Maybe you're not such a numbskull after all."

He drapes his arm around her shoulders, and the two of them lapse into an amiable silence, watching the winking of the city all around them. The honeycombed towers loom high over the theater. Their windows are either bright like fireflies or dark as tombs, and the bright ones seem to be arranging themselves into patterns that are almost recognizable, like the letters of a crude alphabet that is similar, but not quite identical, to his own. Soon, it begins to rain. The steam rises up from the stones on the roof, swelling in clouds around their ankles and separating into opaque plumes as it lifts. It is like all the souls of the city are emerging at once, curling out from the various places they have settled, from the bricks, from the hopscotch sidewalks, from the soot-stained walls of immigrant homes, from the washboards and the stoves and the crockery, from the inherited playthings of children, from the archipelagos of fish offal glistening on the East River boardwalk, from the sewers, from the stiff bridles of ice-wagon horses, even from the great furrowed rocks in Central

Park, whose surfaces were said to have been scarred by an encounter with a monstrous glacier, by that same amalgam of frozen water and sediment that molded Manhattan into its current shape, creeping southward over the span of generations and dragging with it the bones of its epochal prey.

Just two Halloweens ago, Isaac had gone with Asher to a costume party thrown by their loudmouthed friend Jesse, whose father owned a butcher shop and who on several occasions had been seen at school with a gun tucked under his coat. But of course it was not Jesse who made the biggest impression that night.

To begin with, someone brought an oversized jar of white lightning, and the boys got good and drunk on it. Asher alone had three mugs full. Dressed as the Sheik, he spent most of the party dancing suggestively with a girl in a Cleopatra costume, while Isaac, who was swathed in a goofy homemade Roman toga (which he had changed into at the theater—his bubbe would never have agreed to let him participate in a non-kosher holiday), chiefly stayed on the sidelines and flipped cards with the other misfits in the group. Isaac did his best to immerse himself in the game, but his gaze was repeatedly drawn to the spectacle on the dance floor. Asher's white-hot pulse was like a beacon across the room, his animal scent unmistakable even within a crowd.

When it was all over, one of them had suggested that they retire to the roof of the theater, lest they incur the wrath of their respective parents, and so up the stairs they went, stopping on every landing to catch their breath and to give the troubled seas of their stomachs an opportunity to regain equilibrium. Eventually, they burst through the door onto this very roof. While Asher ran excitedly from ledge to ledge, Isaac adopted a more judicious approach, steadying himself and taking in his surroundings from a single vantage point. It was a warm night, and he observed that the buildings across the way were interlaced with veils of freshly hung laundry. In the moonlight the alabaster undergarments shone like pearly scales. He found he was able to tease apart the layers of smoke that filled the air—hickory and maple smoke from the nearby chimney tops, acrid smoke from the foundries across the river, and the occasional draft of heady-sweet smoke that filtered up from someone's cherry tobacco pipe. He was aware, also, of the numinous cries of gulls, keening mournfully in the harbor. And that was when it happened. Out of the corner of his eye he saw a blurred figure approaching, saw his friend rushing at him like a demon in one of those German folk tales, and before he had time to react Asher was dipping him backwards as he had done with the girl at the party, his arm pressed firmly into the center of Isaac's back, supporting him like a second spine. "You cannot resist me," the boy exclaimed, in a rough approximation of an Italian accent, and then proceeded to plant a dramatic stage kiss on Isaac's unprepared lips.

It was astonishing.

Right away the odor of alcohol carried like a garland out of the older boy's mouth and into his own nostrils. There was a hint of something metallic within that vaporous tendril, like the edge of a beer can, and its pungency seemed to endow Isaac with extraordinary vision, so that even through the prism of closed eyelids he could see the high relief of his friend's jaw, could see the dilated green eyes, could see the fall of a striped headdress over a brawny shoulder, and there was Asher's bottom lip brushing ever so slightly against his own, soft, like the wing of a baby bird, and in the convergence of their breath Isaac felt that they were being bound together, that bodies joined by such a tether could not possibly be separated, but would be destined to walk the earth side by side, hip anchored firmly to hip, like those Siamese twins he saw that time at Coney Island, forever fused, sharing their most vital organs, their blood vessels intertwined like a pair of olive trees.

Of course, it was over all too quickly.

After only a moment, Asher lost his balance and let him drop to the ground. He then laughed and began to retreat, lurching away down the stairs, while Isaac lay battered on the stones, marooned, watching in awe as the world dismantled itself before his eyes. Buildings flew apart. Subway tracks unraveled. The East River rose like a black ribbon into the sky. Isaac didn't move a muscle, for fear of shattering the dream. He simply lay where he had fallen, heedful, blissful, until everything around him was gone, until there was nothing left but his frail human form suspended over a vast plain of space, and the sharpened sliver of moon above, which was like a knife curving toward his heart.

At the theater the next day, Asher didn't appear to remember what had happened, or if he did, he didn't feel the incident was anything worth mentioning. "Did you see that hot tomato I was dancing with last night?" he asked Isaac. "She rubbed all up against me while we was close. You know, you ought to get yourself a girl like that, before you settle down with my sister and have lots of boring babies."

And that was that. As far as Asher was concerned, nothing had changed between them. But for months afterward, Isaac was plagued by unexplained bouts of fever that left him feeling vaguely disoriented and mistrustful of his own body. His skin seemed to have become coarse and unfamiliar, like a husk he was temporarily inhabiting. His lips burned like sulfur in the night.

"You know," says Doralee in a quiet voice, without looking at him, "we're a lot the same, him and me. We even look the same. Do you think you could . . . could we maybe . . .? I mean, it's not like we'd have to . . ." She trails off, unable to complete this dangerous thought.

He peers at her, and for once he feels his heart breaking for someone other than himself. "Doralee . . ." he begins.

"No, I suppose not," she says quickly. "I suppose not.

I'm a silly girl is all. Just ignore me, please . . . I don't even know what I'm saying half the time." And then, with the grace of an actress, she slips out from beneath his arm and sweeps gloriously toward the exit, skipping over puddles, her white dress shining, her black patent shoes once again spinning out galaxies. When she has flung open the door, she turns to him one last time, smiling her sweet, dimpled smile, which is broad like a breastplate. "Hey, no offense," she explains, "but this is getting stale, and I've got to meet up with Anka in a few. I'll see you tomorrow, though, right?" She steps backward, a face dissolving into a darkened doorway. He can see that she is waiting for his reply.

"Right," he agrees. "I'll see you tomorrow. By the way, I like your hair. You look just like Louise Brooks."

"Oh thanks, Bunny! Ma wanted me to wait till I was older to get the bob, but I went out and did it anyway. That'll show her!"

And then she is gone, and he is left to ponder everything that has transpired. He finds himself thinking of the last few minutes of *Horsemen*, when the character Julio, having been killed by a shell in no-man's-land, appears to his lover and consoles her. *Small things*, a voice in his head says, although it might just as easily be his own thoughts.

We stay alive for small things. Beauty is reborn.

And so two halves of the same heart turn homeward, one to a mother, one to a long-dead father. An ethereal being folds its essence into the rising vines of steam, slipping back through luminous membranes of space, returning to a realm of wind and sky. And the father receives him with arms that are sinewy with stars. And the mother hugs him fiercely. "I was so afraid for you!" she exclaims, her rumpled dress still smelling of tailor's chalk from the factory. "I had a dream that . . . well, never mind what it was about. I'm just so pleased to see you're okay," and there is his bubbe shaking her copper-wire head and calling her daughter *meshugeneh*, and Little Nate looking up quizzically from his rabbinical textbooks, wondering what all the fuss is about. And the sea-stained walls once more envelop him, with their aging plaster that is reminiscent of a pair of blue-green eyes, or the sort of lagoon from whose waters a well-muscled man might emerge while supporting a racing scull above his head.

And the photographs lie like coiled memories across his cast-iron bed. Though Isaac still feels a pang when he looks at them, the various Valentinos seem to have receded into themselves like a nautilus into its shell—the rajah, the sheik, the matador, each one sequestered within a many-chambered universe. They are now only flat representations of figures, like those that are projected onto a movie screen.

And, for the moment at least, they are just as silent.

STILL LIFE WITH FOSSILS

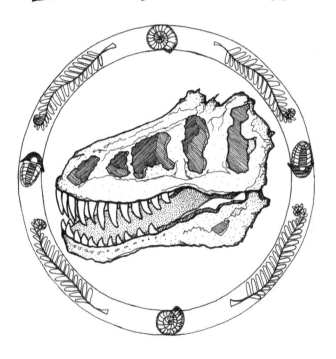

T<small>HE SKELETON OF THE</small> *Tyrannosaurus rex* <small>AWAKES</small> <small>AS IF FROM A DEEP SLUMBER.</small>

He takes in the landscape of his surroundings, expecting to see streams and spongy earth and velvet-green foliage. He expects to be greeted by a bright and blazing sky, and perhaps a nearby nest where others of his kind are congregated. Instead, he finds that he is inside some sort of colossal structure. The ground in this place appears to be hard and smooth. Vivid images are painted on the walls. There are fantastic objects on every side. Below him, there are rocks that he can see right through, rocks that are perfectly flat and symmetrical and that seem to have coalesced around the remains of various organisms. Some of them even contain traditional rocks—rocks buried within rocks?—with the shapes of fish and other water beasts limned into them. Up high, there are holes in the walls that let in light. Strange beacons hang from the roof on what look like ossified vines.

The Tyrannosaurus is thoroughly perplexed. He cannot make sense of any of these things.

Finally, on the next platform over, he notices something that is more familiar to him—the skeleton of a mature dinosaur. This is not an animal that he remembers from his own years of predation, but he has seen enough similar creatures to reasonably guess at its habits and diet. It is a slow and lumbering thing. It engages in herd behavior. It eats only vegetation. And yet, observing its armored body, he can see that it would also make for difficult hunting. One would have to contend with the formidable plates on its back, as well as the massive, spiny tail that would likely sweep up from behind to knock its attacker off balance. He stares at the skeleton, fascinated. How is it that it can remain upright in its current condition? What is holding the pieces together? There are no ligaments, no tendons. How does it not simply collapse into a heap on the ground? He is busy contemplating such questions when he becomes aware of a dull buzzing in the air around him.

At first he believes there must be an insect nearby, one of those nettlesome pests that always seem to crawl inside his nostrils while he is trying to sleep. But then the buzzing undergoes an essential change. It becomes softer, airier of tone, and in general less offensive to the ears, until soon it resolves into a tide of rhythmic susurrations that collectively bear a striking resemblance to language. Though the creature opposite him is only an edifice of bone, it has somehow learned to communicate. Words are issuing from its tiny, unmoving mouth. He can just make out these imprints of sound as they cross the space between the platforms. They are like fleeting exhalations of vapor, and it is with no little puzzlement that the Tyrannosaurus at last realizes he can understand them.

"Welcome, brother," says the creature, whose voice is unmistakably female.

For a long time he is unable to muster even a squeak in response. He is still too awed by his environs, by the inexplicable artifacts that have colonized the ground and hang like tumbled moss from the walls. The only point of security he can locate is that high panel of light, and so he lets his gaze settle onto those lucent, parallel squares, wondering at the source of their radiance, wondering if below this false horizon is the same yellow orb that has illuminated every pursuit of quarry, every tumultuous mating, every milestone of his development since the long-vanished hour of his hatching. He wonders, too, why he is unable to turn his body in one direction or the other. His legs seem to have become a pair of embedded tree trunks within the platform, anchored by the deepest latticework of roots, while his forelimbs are twin branches fixed against the hazy firmament. He cannot even twitch his tail, although he tries repeatedly to do so. To stave off panic, he tells himself that he is only stiff from sleep. He tells himself that his sinews have merely become complacent and need time to return to their old, industrious selves.

After a while he begins to discern that he has his own spectral voice, just like that of the creature across the way. It happens as he is trying to coax a menacing growl from his throat. He just thinks about it and then out it comes, as if a prodigious obstruction of mucus has been cleared away from his larynx. Suddenly the formulation of speech is effortless. Syllables begin to slip from his jaw like so much curling smoke. He asks: "Where . . . where are we?"

"That's rather difficult to say. Our afterlife, I suppose."

"You mean that we aren't alive any longer?"

A silvery laugh emanates from the skeleton (or, more precisely, from the lacunae within it). "Have you taken a look at yourself recently?"

The Tyrannosaurus hesitates for a moment and then glances down at his legs. He is astonished to see that his skin has been removed. That dense, bark-like layer is entirely absent, to say nothing of the muscles beneath it, and now there is only a framework of glossy, petrified stalks representing his body. He can tell right away that this state of disrepair extends all the way up to his head. In particular, he is acutely aware that his eyeballs are missing, although somehow this deficit has not impeded his vision in any meaningful way. As for the rest of him, it seems to have fared little better. There is a curving void where his internal organs used to be. Gone is the beating pulp at his core, as well as the apparatuses for breathing that once flanked it, mysteriously yoked at the center like a dyad of leaves. His genitals are a nullity. His stomach has likewise vacated the premises. Even his brain, the onetime seat of his consciousness, is unaccounted for.

"But . . . how can this be?" he cries. "What happened

to us?" He has fully succumbed to terror now. There is a sudden tightness in his nonexistent throat, as well as the feeling that he has eaten something poisonous, something that needs to be purged at once.

"Aside from the dying, you mean?"

"No . . . well, yes. That is . . . how exactly did we die? Did we starve to death? Was it some kind of combat? I can't remember . . . anything."

The creature waits patiently for him to finish stammering before voicing her reply. "I don't know how you died, brother. All I have is my own story."

At this, the Tyrannosaurus lets out a long, keening howl of despair. It is transported like a fierce wind throughout the room, ascending and descending along every surface of the alien terrain, swirling into plumes, disturbing the peculiar mottled skins that are suspended from the ceiling and causing them to billow out like swells on the open water. Finally, it rushes back to the place where he stands. It threads its way through the solitary prongs of his rib cage, and the movement of air over bone produces a shrill whistling sound that would no doubt have irritated his sensitive ears, had they still been intact. Only when the din has subsided completely does his companion continue with her discourse.

"Just be calm for a moment and think," she instructs him. "What is the last thing you remember before you turned up here?"

He considers the question. But his mind is in turmoil,

and so to begin with he has to clear away the fog, bringing himself to something approximating a tranquil mentality. Only then do the details of his demise begin to emerge. The tableau takes shape, becomes concrete, and as it does he tells himself that the events he witnessed that morning happened not to him, but to another representative of his species. He is therefore able to examine the relevant memories with a fair degree of detachment.

He recalls first that he was on the prowl, scouting for easy prey. There was the lush canopy of green overhead, and the loamy soil underfoot, and the coarse, denticulate fronds that brushed against his neck as he made his way through the forest. There was the smell of a horned herbivore, tantalizing within his nostrils. There was a clearing just beyond the forest where he had hoped to catch up with this tasty bit of provender. Next, he recalls a rumbling that seemed to go on for ages, followed by a deafening boom. He had turned just in time to see a cataclysm of smoke erupting from a nearby mountain. Soon after, a ribbon of red snaked down from the apex and began to carve a sinuous trail through the valley toward him. He recalls staring hard at this glowing filament, trying to ascertain what it was he was seeing. Trying to gauge its distance from him. Trying to determine whether it posed a threat, and if so, whether the threat was an immediate one. The substance was not moving as swiftly as a liquid; it was viscous in nature, moving lazily along its chosen artery, meandering even, as if it had no particular interest in reaching its destination. And then, as it drew closer, he recalls feeling the heat from that molten strand, feeling it singe him even through the shell of his battle-tested epidermis. Blisters were beginning to form on the bottoms of his feet. His eyes stung terribly. His blood seemed in danger of boiling and turning to gas. Lastly, he recalls the primal dread that consumed him as he lurched away from that monstrous rivulet, sprinting in a fever across the shuddering plain, growing more aimless by the second, until he was no longer attending to the hazards in his path, until he had stumbled into a deep and sticky pit from which he was simply unable to extricate himself.

He imparts all of this to the entity beside him, including even those elements that expose his temporary cowardice. He figures there is no point in trying to safeguard his dignity when he has been stripped of everything else.

The creature listens attentively to his story. She makes sympathetic noises from time to time, and when he is finished, she begins to confide her own remarkable tale of misery. Her account is not so different from his, minus the fiery spectacle. She'd been attempting to sniff out water when she was enveloped by the same glutinous mass that had absorbed him. Slowly it drew her into itself. Swimming across it was impossible, and struggling to free herself only made matters worse. There were no footholds, no rocks or other detritus to stand on, nothing to keep her from being fully submerged in the mire. She was sinking, and that was that. (Even in this predicament, she was able to appreciate the cleverness of such a snare. Here was an organism that could deliquesce on command, employing its own body as a trap to capture food. In other words, it was the perfect predator.)

Her voice becomes low and conspiratorial as she describes what happened next. Her head had just slipped beneath the jetty goo. Her lungs were screaming for air, and her body had begun to convulse. Instinctively, then, she opened her eyes. That was when she saw them: plants, birds, insects, animals of every kind, an entire floating graveyard of specimens that had once proliferated in the world beyond. None of them had undergone any sort of decay; they were all miraculously preserved exactly as they had been at the moment of their deaths. She saw other things, too. Impossible things. Against the backdrop of blackness she saw her favorite drinking pond as it was before it dried up; she saw her nest from when she was a youngling; she saw her brothers and sisters scrambling through the brush and discovering the strength of their legs; she even saw her mother, with her distinct and beautiful back plates; and everything she saw was wreathed in its own scintillant aura, as if it were caught in the radiance of an exceptionally bright morning.

"I didn't see any such thing," says the Tyrannosaurus

skeptically. "I just thrashed around for a while and then went to sleep."

"I know it sounds unlikely, but it was absolutely clear to me at the time. I also heard a voice, assuring me that I would see the others again, in some subsequent life."

"The others?"

"I had little ones, you know," she says, her skeletal visage giving the distinct impression of a frown. "I don't know what happened to them."

The Tyrannosaurus chuckles. "Well they're dead, no doubt. I get the feeling it's been more than a few lifetimes since we last saw our skins." And then, realizing that he has said the wrong thing, he adds: "But I'm sure your babies lived a long time and didn't get eaten."

This elicits another ethereal laugh from the creature, albeit one that is more halfhearted than the first. "Very kind of you to say, brother. Of course, back then you would have tried to eat my entire family for your evening meal."

"Yes, well, we are beyond such things now," he responds awkwardly.

He remembers, nevertheless, the raw and pungent odor of fresh blood. He remembers the desire to track, to feast, to kill. It is like a red flag flickering in the place where his brain used to be. He can feel it pulsing in his jaw as well, bound within the porous spaces of his petrified teeth. What is he to do from now on? His existence has always been structured around the acquisition of food, but the only prey in the vicinity is a curiously humped creature without any meat left on her frame, and he is not particularly interested in attacking her, not even if they were both made whole again and he had the means of ambulation. A hunter is defined in opposition to the thing he hunts, so what does that make him? What other identity could he possibly assume at this late stage?

"Very true," the creature is saying. "Carnivore or no, it seems we all end up in the same place."

"And what place is that?"

"The world as it is today."

"So if we aren't alive, then what exactly are we?"

She takes a deep breath, considering her answer. "We are a lingering dream," she replies at last. "We are the fragment of our consciousness that didn't die when our bodies did, but instead became embedded within our own bones. Held inside by whatever alchemical ointment they've used to keep us from falling apart. You see, our spirits aren't really separate from our physical selves. They are intertwined in some essential way, which is why we are able to have this conversation in the first place. But it won't be like this forever, I assure you. After a season, the voice that I heard will come and collect us and take us somewhere more permanent. Somewhere more peaceful, and without the appalling sense of tedium."

"How long have you been waiting here?"

"I have no perception of time having passed. What

I do know is that I've seen more of *those* things than I have the wherewithal to count."

The Tyrannosaurus follows her gaze and is flabbergasted to see yet another exotic animal, this time one that is fully upright. Unlike him, it is still in possession of its outer sheath. It has arms and legs, both of unusual proportion (the former are quite long and the latter quite short). It has fur, too, but only on the crest of its head. The scales on its upper torso are a forest green, and its lower half is encased in a pelt of dark blue. Most notably, it can move. It is not fixed in space like some topographical irregularity, it is not held captive within its own anatomy—it is not dead. The animal comes to stand directly in front of his platform and gazes up at him without fear. This strikes him as disrespectful in the extreme.

He wonders if the animal is posturing for a turf battle, and the thought amuses him until he remembers a crucial fact: namely, that the incongruity in their sizes is no longer of any consequence. He is now a stationary object. If the interloper truly intends to displace him, there is nothing he can do to prevent the action.

The animal soon turns away and begins to generate a string of foreign intonations, which the Tyrannosaurus decides must be a kind of language, although to him it sounds like nothing more than stones being scraped against one another. This is when he realizes that there are other such animals nearby. In truth, they are everywhere. Shifting, circulating, examining the relics. Converging in clouds and then dispersing like vapor. The younglings are describing wide orbits around the elders, while the elders occupy themselves with their eccentric stone-speech. He notices that no two animals are endowed with the same husk. Their exteriors vary in shape and coverage, and in terms of pigmentation, they seem to cast up every shade in the visible spectrum. He cannot help but be impressed by the sheer numbers of the herd. Just when he thinks he has seen them in their totality, more of the animals begin to trickle in through the twin openings in the far wall.

"What the devil are they?"

"They're what's here instead of us."

"You mean they're the dominant form of life?" he asks, incredulous. It doesn't seem plausible. These animals look ill-equipped to survive, what with their soft exteriors and notable lack of weaponry. Their talons are tiny. Impractical. How do they fight? And perhaps more to the point, how could they possibly have defeated the larger, grander beasts of the earth? How could they be flourishing when he and those like him have become a wrecked species, enduring only as lineaments of memory, their flesh dissolved, their bodies shrunk to a brittle latticework of ruin?

"I'm afraid so, brother. Not the most auspicious-looking group, are they?"

"I should say not."

One of the animals approaches him, carrying a small

gray object that appears to be a morsel of food. Instead of eating it, however, it places the item over its eyes and holds it there for several seconds. The Tyrannosaurus is mystified by this behavior. He is beginning to question the animal's sanity, when suddenly he finds himself dazzled by a flash of light. It obscures his vision completely. All he can see is a starburst of sorts, a nimbus of incandescence, which soon splinters into a hundred geometric patterns before his eyes, each one resembling a cobweb, or a sea coral, or the multipronged head of a flower. He is outraged—he believes that he has been struck blind. But then he hears the creature's silvery laugh from the adjacent platform, and within moments the world begins to filter back into focus. Opacity lifts like a fog. His sight is restored.

He thinks he understands now why these animals have fared as well as they have through the years. They are clever. Inventive. They have learned to compensate for their diminutive size by creating useful devices that can manipulate their environments in a way that he and his kind never could have dreamed of. He has to admire their resourcefulness. Still, his encounter with the gray object has left him feeling irritable. "So why do they come here?" he demands. "Just to taunt us with their light boxes?"

"I get the impression that they built this place," the creature replies. "I do know that they are the ones who found our bones in the ground, affixed them to one another, and then set us out to be viewed like this. I can't say why exactly—it must have something to do with the way they instruct their offspring. They appear to value knowledge of the past."

The Tyrannosaurus snorts at this notion. "Seems like knowledge of the future would be more helpful," he says. He is thinking of the flaming mountain and the treacherous pit and his own ignominious end. "Anyway, how does standing here and gawking at us prepare their young for the demands of survival? How does it help them scavenge for food? How does it help them find unpolluted water? How does it help them protect themselves from enemies?"

"I think maybe they don't have enemies."

"That's . . . absurd."

"What's your explanation then? Only animals without enemies would have the leisure to construct things as immense as this shelter. And what about putting us back together, piece by piece? That had to have taken a good deal of time, which wouldn't have been possible if there were bloodthirsty beasts hunkering nearby, just waiting for the opportunity to sink their teeth into those vulnerable little necks."

He can't think of a good response to this. He glances around him, surveying the ebb and flow of animals throughout the room. Their constant motion fascinates him. They surge with almost botanical exuberance, occupying every corner, every niche, as if the idea of untenanted space is hateful to them, as if emptiness itself is a thing meant to be conquered and driven from the earth.

These are animals that do not negotiate. They devour in ways that he never did. He can tell by the manner in which they migrate from one artifact to the next, exhibiting a zeal that goes beyond the fulfillment of physical need, beyond what is required for pure subsistence. Rather, they thrive on something else, something visceral and intangible. They are infinitely curious. He suspects that they are also dangerous. "I wonder," he muses, "did the voice mention anything about them? Do they have their own place like this? For after they die?"

"I don't know—the voice only told me about my own prospects. Who's to say what will happen to those things once they meet their own extinction? Who knows whether they even experience consciousness in the same sense that we do? Perhaps they are more akin to high-functioning plants, and there is not so much as a scrap of sentience left over after they die."

"But they're very intelligent."

"What does that have to do with anything?" she asks. She is clearly relishing their exchange, and it occurs to him how lonely it must have been to have emerged into this cryptic region without a guide, or at least someone to talk to. It's no wonder the creature is so eager to enmesh herself in an ontological debate with whoever happens to be present.

"Well, I would have thought that intelligence had *something* to do with it," he suggests.

"That's because you're interpreting events based solely on your perceived taxonomy of the world. The potential for some form of vital essence doesn't necessarily increase or decrease commensurate to your place on the food chain, you know. Although, let's face it, that's the only real indicator of intelligence our kind can fathom."

"You may be right. I'd wager they're too small to have a vital essence anyway. Where would it be stashed in such a tiny vessel?

"Just so."

"Then I guess we're on our own, biding our time here until this elusive voice of yours gathers us under its unseen wing and transports us to our final rest. Which brings to mind another question—what exactly is the purpose of all this waiting?"

"Perhaps we're meant to use this interval to reflect on our lives."

"I fail to see the benefit of that, now that we're dead. Besides, what would we rectify, if we had it all to do over again? We lived according to our biological imperatives. I could decide to become an herbivore like you, but I wouldn't last five days eating only ferns and twigs. My body was designed to run on a more substantial kind of fuel. Likewise, I'm sure you did as your instinct dictated. You foraged, you found a nest, you took care of your babies. What could you have done differently?"

Now it is the creature's turn to be stumped. "Fair enough," she concedes.

She adopts a pensive expression. As she loses herself in another period of reverie, the Tyrannosaurus imagines that he can see the delicate current of her thoughts, looping like a thin, pearly fiber through her half-crescent form. He conceives of a lovely iridescence, coiling around her spine; arcing upward into her back plates; permeating, even, the sleek scaffolding of her bones. He is thus occupied when she finally responds. "I don't have an answer for you, brother. I suppose we just have to trust that there is a reason."

He could argue with this, but he chooses not to.

And so begins the slow drift of days, the perpetual succession of light and of darkness, in which time can be measured largely by what is seen through those rectangular panels overhead, whether it be clumps of red-gold leaves exfoliated by the surrounding trees, or motes of white falling in a gossamer curtain. Sometimes the panels are fogged over. Sometimes they are clear, revealing flocks of birds in a ragged "V" formation. The passing of equinoxes is further marked by corresponding changes in the animals' appearance. Their coats prove to be highly adaptable, growing longer or shorter, heavier or lighter, in accordance with the altered weather conditions.

Years elapse. Decades even. And still the Tyrannosaurus and his companion await their liberation. For the sake of sanity they learn to be wholly candid with each other. She tells him how she misses the humidity of their world, the sultry, fog-thick air, and how the dryness in this place feels to her like an absence of atmosphere, as if at any moment she might lose contact with the ground and be drawn upward into the bright funnel of sky.

She tells him how she used to love walking through the velutinous underbrush, and immersing her whole body in water. She tells him also all about her little ones, about their singular features and habits, how it felt to awaken in the nest with them squirming beside her, warm and smelling of berries.

He tells her about a fight he once had with a competitor that caused his tail to become damaged. He mourns the loss of movement, describing in elegiac tones the masterful articulation of his toes. He remembers a thorn that had been wedged deep in his foot for days before working itself out. Whenever a particularly interesting animal happens by, they trade fanciful suppositions about its origins. The one in green rose up whole from a bed of moss. The one with the wrinkled exterior must have been birthed by a fish. He comes to treasure the creature's silvery laugh.

At last comes the point where they have fallen silent, having told each other everything, disclosed every thought, every observation, concerning both past and present. What remains is a comforting quiescence, in which they are able to simply exist and be glad of each other's company. Their awareness begins to lie dormant for days at a time. During these interludes they become mere simulacra of their earlier selves. Their voices and vibrations are suspended. Their independent ruminations are cast off, until they have transformed into parallel branches of the same ancient tree, with bark hewed from bone and roots as deep as the world.

One morning he rouses from such a period of hibernation to see that the creature is gone. He can find no sign of her. The platform where she stood is empty, except for a few unfamiliar gadgets and what appears to be a fine coating of silt-brown powder. He can just make out a pattern amid the detritus—four small imprints where her tiny feet had been. The outlines are perfect and unsmudged. It is as if she has been lifted directly upward. Soon he becomes aware of a slight haze in the vicinity as well, a temporal veil of unsettled particles. But where he would expect to smell mustiness there is only the faint, sweet odor of flora, as if an invisible garland were diffusing its fragrance throughout the room.

It is a poignant development, and for a while he is hopelessly distraught, unable to reconcile himself to her absence. He cannot imagine what he will do without her. It surprises him how dependent he has become on her quiet ubiquity, on her tranquil, self-assured demeanor and her wry disposition. Most of all, however, he has come to depend on the knowledge of her specific past as a sort of anchor for his own mercurial memories.

With her gone, how will he know that he still exists? That he ever really did?

But the hours keep cycling by, and even grief is ephemeral. Eventually his gloom subsides. It falls away like so many scales, like the night he wandered into a thicket of bramble bushes and left pieces of his skin behind. What he is left with now is a new hide, comprised of new cells and new thoughts. New perspectives. Alone, he continues within the dream, only half-attuned to the sights and sounds of his immediate environment, the present commingling with the past, so that the walls begin to reverberate with Pteranodon cries and the relic cases are overrun with marine plants. It would be fair to say that he has an appendage in each world. He moves through time as if through water, navigating both upstream and downstream, until a day comes when another skeletal creature materializes beside him in that strange place, standing in utter bewilderment on the adjoining platform and doing his best to comprehend his surroundings.

The new arrival is one that he recognizes at once from his former life—a Triceratops. He knows the beast by its heft, and by its body length, which is a bit more truncated than that of his erstwhile associate. He knows it by its prominent horns and its massive halo of frill. He knows it because he has hunted and eaten such creatures on countless occasions. He can remember precisely how the thing tasted, how the scent of its blood rose up in a burgeoning cloud all around him as he fed. He can remember the ease with which its flesh came dissevered from bone.

And yet, the Tyrannosaurus can't help but feel a sense of kinship with this most recent refugee from prehistory. He knows its dazed expression all too well. His own previous confusion is reflected in its wild-eyed aspect (conveyed impressively by a pair of empty ocular cavities), and in the smooth curve of its back, which is arched like a question. He gives it a moment to collect its bearings. And then, clearing his insubstantial throat, he adjusts his voice to what he hopes will be a reassuring timbre.

"Welcome, brother," he says, and settles in to wait for a reply.

THE
PISCINE AGE

MARGITA STOOD WITH HER HANDS PRESSED AGAINST THE SCREEN DOOR, LOOKING OUT INTO THE BLACKNESS OF A COOL SUMMER'S NIGHT. The stars were out in their milky multitudes. Like tiny pearls, they glimmered behind the aluminum veil of the grid. She saw that they were especially profuse in the upper-right-hand corner where the mesh had begun to come loose, curling back on itself like the membrane of some hidden universe, exposing a secret triangle of space through which rogue particles of dark matter —to say nothing of the duskywing moths—could enter their home. She gazed a moment longer and then closed the door.

As usual, Ben was asleep in the bathtub.

"Wake up, babe. Wake up. How are you feeling?"

Ben responded with a deep, guttural yawn that seemed to go on for minutes. "Hey," he said at last, grinning up at her. "I feel all right."

"How's the water? Do you need more bath oil?"

"Yeah . . . it looks that way. It's just not having much effect anymore."

A quick survey of his legs and torso confirmed this; the region was just as dry and scabrous as ever. Nothing, it seemed, could push back the slow tide of his transformation. A thousand tiny conquests had left his lower body as it was now, vanquished, submerged beneath a patchwork of scales, which glittered in the water like sea glass and sent out signal jets whenever he moved. Margita let out a small sigh and rested her hand on the comparatively smooth skin of his shoulder. "I was afraid of that," she murmured.

BEN AND MARGITA LIVED IN MAIDEN'S CAPE, A SMALL coastal town in Oregon at the western edge of Tillamook County. She was forty-three, he was forty-five, and they had been married for just over fifteen years. For most of that time Ben had been healthy, suffering mainly from higher-than-average blood pressure and the occasional flare-up of hemorrhoids. His childhood had been similarly incident free; despite a certain wildness of upbringing, he had never even broken a bone. In fact, the past eleven months marked the first time in his life that he had been seriously ill.

It had started with a simple rash. During their last visit to Hell's Canyon, a small patch of pustules had appeared on the callused soles of Ben's feet, like a tiny wreath of roses at the center of each arch. Believing it to be either poison oak or poison ivy, Margita had dabbed it with rubbing alcohol, cleansed it with soap and water, and kept it covered with gauze pads, just as her father had taught her to do. But the rash refused to dissipate, and in the weeks that followed its appearance underwent a startling transformation. The color shifted from red to brown, from brown to blue, and finally from blue to a deep, dusky violet. The pustules burst and flattened, leaving behind skin that was hard like armor. And then the breakout began to spread. It climbed up his legs, circling the flesh slowly like pestilent Maypole ribbons, before proliferating across his lower trunk and radiating down the tender stalk of his penis. Its progress finally halted at the level of his waist, a cessation that brought both relief and horror as they marveled at what he had become. The expanse of his lower body was a parched wasteland, amethyst in color, and oddly tessellated.

At the hospital, Ben endured countless hours of examination. With Margita at his side, he was probed with needles, biopsied, given a full battery of allergen tests, and inspected from head to toe for the presence of cutaneous parasites. When these diagnostics failed, he gamely submitted himself to the care of a team of dermatological specialists in Portland, one of whom was on loan from the Mayo Clinic. These experts administered tests for staph infection, folliculitis, psoriasis, lichen planus, lichen sclerosus, pityriasis, skin cancer, and even leprosy. In the end, though, they couldn't arrive at any kind of consensus regarding his condition.

"Our best guess is ichthyosis," explained his physician, Dr. Molloy, with her wire-rimmed spectacles pushed low on her patrician nose. "We can't say for sure, though, since none of the forms fit your symptoms perfectly."

Ben had to laugh at this. "Well hell," he said. "I always was a nonconformist."

Dr. Molloy went on to warn the couple about the potential for contagion. She recommended that they sleep in separate beds, that the laundry and dishes be done on a daily basis, and that Margita wear gloves whenever she touched her husband, even on those areas unaffected by the rash. But although they nodded politely at everything she said, they had no intention of altering their daily routine to include these precautions. (If the condition were truly communicable, wouldn't Margita have caught it already?) The other major prohibition, of course, was sex, and in this case the doctor's argument was purely an academic one. Sex in the traditional sense had been impossible for months. To begin with they had contented themselves with manual stimulation, but given that Ben's member was busy plating itself in thick, purplish scales, the friction had eventually proved to be too painful for him. Since then they had found ways to sublimate.

They had taught themselves to kiss all over again. They had renamed their body parts after galaxies. They had learned to curl up in the big stuffed-leather chair, beneath the painting of St. Andrew on the cross, and cling to one another as if floating among the debris of a shipwreck. Sometimes they held their breaths and imagined the slow circling of sharks. Ben would sing the mariners' ballads his father had taught him. Margita would fold her arms around his chest, as if by grasping him tightly enough, she could hold her husband fixed in time, delaying or even reversing the progress of his illness.

The only known treatment for ichthyosis was hydration of the skin, and so the couple embarked on a search for the ideal topical regimen. Under Dr. Molloy's guidance, they experimented with a variety of medicated creams. When these proved inadequate, they moved on to over-the-counter moisturizers. These, they were free to use as liberally as they liked. Ben would stand on the bath rug, arms jutting out like a scarecrow's, while Margita ministered to his trunk and legs using ever more copious amounts of lotion. This method brought immediate relief (as well as frequent, uncomfortable erections), but the effects were not long-lived. Ben's newly armored skin was insatiable. It thirstily absorbed the creams, so that by the time Margita reached his feet, the chitinous plating around his waist would have returned, a brutish secret that could not be contained.

Next they tried a variety of alternative remedies. Honey liniments. Beeswax. Cotton balls soaked with benzyl alcohol. Margita kept a detailed journal of her husband's response to each solution, and dutifully reported it to the doctor on every visit. The documentation functioned as a kind of therapy for her. Even after they stopped going to the clinic she continued the practice, finding it was the most reliable way to soothe her mounting fears. (Naturally, Dr. Molloy had not wanted to lose such a fascinating patient. She had phoned them on a daily basis, urging them to recon-sider, until at last Margita had had enough of the in-trusions. "Can't you just leave him in peace?" she cried. "My husband does not want to be poked and prodded for the rest of his life.")

Several weeks after that phone call, they happened upon the most effective remedy of all, the keratolytic bath.

But by then Ben's legs had started to fuse together.

"Looks like your blouse is wet," Ben teased, and pulled his wife into the tub with him. She shrieked with laughter, flailing, punching him playfully until he found her mouth and began breathing into it, supplant-ing the air in her lungs with his own. It was amazing how strong he was now. Amazing how the sinews in his arms had grown large after months of dragging his legs and trunk behind him. His biceps were grapefruits that bobbed beneath the skin. His forearms were dense like wood, and when he flexed, the muscles rippled across his back like rogue ocean currents. From the waist up, he looked like one of those wrestlers she saw on late-night television. From the waist up, it was easy to forget anything was wrong.

As a child, Margita had loved to climb the lofty mulberry trees that flanked her house. She perched in them as in an aerie, tracing ornate pictographs against the twilight spaces, fashioning new constellations and naming them after friends and favorite book characters. Such impulses had never really left her. Even now, she dreamed of nebulas. Even now, she was made delirious by the movement of planets.

When she discovered that Ben shared her fascination with the night sky, it was as if a lamp had been placed inside his chest. His skin suddenly appeared translucent to her. His eye sockets were converted into tunnels of light.

This had happened at the Tillamook County Fair, their first date, and as they walked the rows of fishing booths and ring toss stalls they dared each other to name as many constellations as they could. Orion. Andromeda. Pegasus. Ara. In the end, Margita had triumphed, summoning "Triangulum" from the foggy depths of memory. To signal his surrender, Ben bought her a celebratory corn dog and kissed her on the lips.

By this time, an aura of impenetrable intimacy hung over them. On the Ferris wheel, they whispered and giggled and clutched at each other like teenagers. Margita was especially enamored with his wavy, straw-colored hair. Because he worked on the docks, unloading crates of fish and lobster, his shaggy locks were heavily imbued with the scent of ocean. It was so pungent that she wondered if the physical properties of his hair had changed after so many years of working in such proximity to the water, so that the proteins and keratin were now permanently spliced with salt. Not that she minded the smell. There was something exhilarating about it. It made her think of trade winds and pitch-soaked timber and barnacles pressed between fingernails. (Later, when they had removed their clothes, she would marvel that the scent remained: a veritable cloud of brine, curling out from his body like tentacles.) It was in that rickety gondola that she first felt a certainty about him. With each rocking of the cart she seemed to see a shutter opening and closing beneath them, revealing frames of their life together in rapid motion. It was all there, the engagement, the wedding, the honeymoon, the moments of quotidian bickering and conjugal felicity. But there was a sharp glare obscuring the content of the later scenes, as if the images had been damaged. And so she pledged herself without foreknowledge, her legs swinging out into nothing.

From that day on, they were inseparable. They took hikes, prepared meals together, pored over star charts. In the evenings they would go to the beach at Tillamook Bay. They would roll out the old army blanket and lounge there for hours, curled up among the plastic relics left by the vacationers. In these moments they were truly at the mercy of the infinite. The blaze of stars seemed to scorch their skin. The sand burrowed into their pores, gently seeding their bodies for pearls. When they could no longer resist, they let themselves fall into that endless plane of grayish black, let themselves be smoothed out over the expanse of the waves, like a bolt of fabric unrolling, so that at no point were the fibers thick enough to contain the full amplitude of their bliss.

The necessity of work proved only a minor obstacle to the lovers. Ben called Margita twice a day at her clerk's desk at City Hall, and every day at noon they ate lunch together down at the docks. When they were apart, they searched for traces of each other within everyday objects. In the office bathroom, Margita saw Ben's features reflected in the contour of the faucet (his gently curving spine), in the seashell soap dish (his ammonite ears), and in the decorative whorls that adorned the wallpaper (his untamable cowlick). And on alternate Saturdays, while Ben was running the grinder at the pulp mill, he observed that the light pouring through the east-facing windows transformed each spray of wood chips into an explosion of celestial shards —a veritable fountain of suns—which came close to capturing the radiance of Margita's gold-flecked eyes.

It seemed to them that the whole world was in league with their love. It sprouted signs within ripened fields and across fertile valleys. It grew gravid with portents.

The first night of their honeymoon, they camped in a dewy autumn meadow with their secondhand telescope so as to better observe the Hale-Bopp comet. They were not disappointed. To the naked eye, the comet appeared as an ethereal smudge of brightness against the black; through the lens, however, it was like a luminous thumbprint, almost too beautiful to be apprehended. When Ben began to stroke the fine hairs on the nape of her neck, Margita was afraid that her organs would simultaneously rupture with happiness.

Of course, this was all in the years before Ben's illness. These days even the simplest outings required hours of diligent preparation. Further complicating matters was his recent decision to venture out of the house only under cover of darkness, lest he attract unwanted attention from their inquisitive neighbors. To be sure, it was a frustrating situation. But although Margita sometimes resented having to play the nurse, that tired stereotype of female domesticity, she found that she couldn't stay angry with her husband for long. After all, it wasn't his fault what was happening to his body.

BEN AND MARGITA WERE SOAKED TO THE BONE. THEY had exhausted themselves with horseplay, reaching that inevitable point where physical considerations forced them to stop; or rather, where they were able to proceed, but in a purely one-sided fashion. Ben's hands slipped into the water, seeking her out. Since they had had to reinvent their lovemaking, Margita's skin had become acutely responsive to his touch. It seemed raw somehow, prone to gooseflesh, like skin that had been grown in a laboratory. It was stirred to sensation so easily it was almost painful. She rolled back against him, a fish on its hook, and as she did so she felt the crow's feet erasing themselves, the ghosts of gray vanishing from her hair, the breasts swelling and becoming firm beneath his touch. Age spots lifted from her arms like fruit flies. Varicose veins submerged. Her once-chapped lips grew moist and florid. Even her vision began to improve, so that before long she could see things once veiled by skeins of solid matter. Behind the wallpaper there was a single lacework plank, a ruin left by long-dead termites. Above the ceiling, a jeweled sky.

When she came, there was the simultaneous pang of melancholy tinged with guilt. It wasn't enough to have gratification for her own body. She wanted to be a mirror, to reflect her raptures back at her husband. She wanted him to feel every luminous wavelength for himself.

Relaxing at last, Ben draped a languid arm around her neck. "Have I told you how beautiful you look today? If not, consider it noted."

Margita laughed, settling in against him. The pungent scent of his fingers was oddly comforting, like vapors from a hearth that had been built just for her. "Beautiful. Right. Me and my ever-spreading ass."

"I, for one, don't care if it spreads. I think our asses get more interesting as we age. They develop character. Anyway, look what's going on with *mine* as of late. It's like something out of a reptile exhibit."

Margita grinned and tousled his sandy hair. "You

know," she observed, "the poet types are always carrying on about the joys of growing old together. But damned if they don't leave out most of the pertinent details."

BEN'S FATHER, A FISHERMAN BY TRADE, HAD SUB- scribed to the full array of nautical superstitions. He was wary of unlucky Fridays; fearful of shooting an albatross or casting stones overboard; and unwilling to trim his hair, beard, or fingernails until the ship that ferried him was safely docked. He had a healthy respect for sharks and the flotsam of omens that bloomed in their wakes. He believed in mermaids, in sea monsters, in the fabled realm of Fiddler's Green. And he spoke in whispers of the mysterious Bermuda Triangle, where he believed it was his destiny to die.

"One day," he confided to his son across the dinner table, "that place will come to claim me. Then you'll have to be a brave and self-sufficient boy and take care of things on your own." It didn't matter that those co- ordinates lay on the other end of the continent from where his job took him. Here was a man who under- stood that the sea was not always linear, that at any moment it might draw you into its eddy, transporting you to waters far away and dark.

(Ben had never known what to make of this declara- tion, especially after his father's long-liner was lost in a freak storm near Grayland. Not so much as a lanyard was recovered.)

But if Ben's father had been a creature of infinite possibilities while at sea, then on land he was an unwavering traditionalist. He maintained a firm schedule: meals were at seven, eleven, and four o'clock sharp; bedtime was at eight (at least for Ben); and the morning alarm went off at five thirty. He tolerated little in the way of whimsy. Ben was not allowed to tell riddles or jokes, and if he was caught indulging in make-believe he was punished with the belt. Thus, Ben spent his early years inhabiting two distinct selves. When his father was at home, Ben had to watch his every move, subsisting in a claustrophobic zone of structure and discipline. But when his father was away, he was left entirely to his own devices, fixing his own meals, sleeping and rising whenever he liked, riding dirt bikes with his friends in the afternoons and getting into mischief in the evenings. The only hint of adult supervision was the weekly visit from their neighbor Mrs. Crowley, who checked in to make sure he hadn't burned the place down.

Perhaps the greatest thrill for the boy was watching his father's ship come in, even though it meant an end to freedom and a return to routine. He loved to stand on the docks alongside the squawking gulls, while the chilly salt wind electrified his flesh and sent ripples of pleasure down his arms. When he first caught sight of it, out there among the distant billows, it was a mere cipher on the horizon, the faintest suggestion of an aquatic shape.

He liked to pretend it was a ghost ship making its final, silent voyage to the afterworld, and he would bless its passing with a bit of Latin (learned from a Catholic classmate). *Dies irae, dies illa, solvet saeculum in favilla.* Little by little the vessel would draw closer to shore. It seemed to assemble itself before his very eyes: boards flying together, plank attaching to oiled plank, the hull growing gradually wider, the keel sinking deeper beneath the waves. At last it would come sailing into Tillamook Bay with its brimming hauls of crab and salmon and tuna, and whenever the boy saw those volumes of scuttling cargo being brought ashore, he was sure that *this* time his father had done it. This time he had emptied the ocean.

The man had spoken of Ben's mother on just one occasion, and his speech had been so slurred by whiskey that it was difficult to understand him. Ben gleaned only that she had somehow saved him from drowning, miles from the nearest shore.

"Bullshit," Margita whispered, and pressed a finger over his lips to silence him.

Ben squeezed her tighter. He had known this would be her reaction. For a while the couple just lay still in the tepid water, their arms interwoven, their bodies curling like smoke around each other. Ben took the opportunity to look closely at his wife.

He observed the spots and the veins, the settling

breasts, the extra portion of cellulite around the hips (though he didn't mind those things nearly as much as she thought he did). He admired her smooth belly, and the way the tips of her wet hair formed angel-whorls against her delicate neck. Next, he found himself listening to their commingled breathing. Their respirations were unmistakably organic; they waxed and waned like the wind, elemental in essence, susurrant, comprising a sinuous double helix of sound that stood in sharp contrast to the metronomic drip-drip-drip of the kitchen tap. Ten minutes elapsed. When at last he felt her frame relax against him, he decided to try again, this time employing a slightly different tactic. He put on his softest, most soothing voice—the one he used when she was snoring and he wanted to tell her to roll over without waking her. "Look, babe," he began. "My legs are so brittle I can hardly get around at all anymore."

"That's what the wheelchair's for," Margita responded curtly.

"But it's just a temporary fix. The fact is, my legs are in pain all the time now—more pain than I've ever let on about. You've seen the scales break off, right? Well, when that happens the skin underneath is basically an open sore. It's raw and burning and it hurts like hell until it eventually hardens and forms another scale, which then goes on to do the same thing. The only time I feel any relief is here in the bathtub, and even that isn't helping as much as it used to."

"I know you're in pain," she said, exasperated. "I know that. But maybe we can find something else that will help. We haven't tried every emollient in the world, you know."

"I think we have," he laughed. "There are trophy wives in Beverly Hills who would kill for my skin-care regimen."

"So we go back to the doctor. We see if there's something else she can tell us, some new experimental therapy we can try."

"No, no, no. I'm done with all of that. At this point I'd like to hold on to what little dignity I have left."

"But why tomorrow? Surely another couple of weeks wouldn't hurt."

"No, Margita," he reiterated quietly, and stroked her dark hair. "No. It has to be tomorrow. Before it's too late."

She half-turned to look at him, taking this answer in. He could feel the slow blaze of her temper like a physical presence in the room, spiraling steadily, ever higher, until it reached its inexorable boiling point.

"Why are you doing this?" she exploded at last. "Why are you giving up after all this time? Are you tired of me? Is that it? Is that why it's so easy for you to throw away our life together? Well, screw that. Maybe I'm tired of you, too. Maybe I hate you and I think you're a selfish piece of shit."

That was when he lost his patience. "Christ, Margita, it's not like there's going to be some kind of medical miracle taking place here. You think *this*—(he paused to gesture at his conjoined legs)—is going to just spontaneously reverse itself? You think I'm going to wake up one morning and the scales will have disappeared, and everything will be bright and pretty and covered with rainbows? You're dreaming, honey. That is not going to happen. So what is it you want from me? You want me to ignore the fact that most days it feels like my skin is being ripped from the bone? You want me to be some kind of martyr for you? The thing is, I have a choice here. I can deal with this problem, and I can do it with some small amount of grace, or I can live in painful denial for however long I have left, which isn't likely to be very long anyway. Not everybody gets a choice, you know."

"Yes, lucky you," she spat. "Maybe you should go to Vegas or something."

Then she rested her head against the arc of his shoulder and began to cry. Of course, he melted. He had always melted when she cried, even the very first few times, when they had been married for only a few weeks and she had gone through that paranoid phase where she was convinced that he was having an affair. She had wept bitterly, he remembered, and every time he had embraced her and said, "I'm not cheating on you, crazy lady. You're confusing me with your old boyfriends." Not that he could blame her for her occasional preoccupation with the past. Ben's high school sweetheart had nearly overdosed on sleeping pills one time after a fight, and as a result he had a tendency to become uneasy whenever Margita was in the bathroom for longer than a few minutes. He couldn't help himself. At the five-minute mark he would begin to knock quietly, and she, in turn, would begin to tease him. "Give me a second, babe," she'd say. "I'm adjusting the noose." All he could do was laugh and go back to his crime shows. Perhaps, Ben thought, people never really got rid of their ghosts. Perhaps they could only learn to live with them, like inconsiderate roommates who made too much noise in the night.

He gazed down at himself then, tracing the star that was tattooed just beneath his heart (hand-inked by one of his buddies from the pulp mill). As it had aged, the edges had begun to curl up, starfish-like. It occurred to him that his whole body was now in on the mutiny. Even his feet, which had begun to turn steadily outward, like fins.

FOR A WHILE HE HAD BEEN ABLE TO CAMOUFLAGE the problem with blue jeans. They had gone out just like usual to the supermarket, to the beach, to the video store, to their favorite seafood restaurant, and although he lumbered a bit like a mummy in a horror movie, no one was the wiser for it. (If anyone was brazen enough to ask, Ben would attribute the stiffness to early-onset arthritis.)

To further protect her husband's secret, Margita always waited until nightfall to drive him to the ocean for his restorative swims. In a way these outings were hopelessly romantic. There they were with their arms draped around each other, their bodies battered by the tides, delirious, yearning, out of control. It was as if nothing material existed beyond the scope of their embrace. The seaweed coiled itself into love-knots around their ankles. The water was cold and curative (and not just for Ben, either; Margita was just starting to inherit the soreness in her joints that was so common among women in her family). Even the moon hung over them like some sort of prop, like there was a stagehand behind the horizon whose job it was to dangle the orb from a fishing pole, drawing it slowly across the sky so as to remind them that time was still moving, that they were not children anymore, not even young lovers, but middle-aged spouses whose unabated affection for each other was considered by the townsfolk to be wildly inappropriate. "Love's like any other seasoning," said Mrs. Tulley, who ran the bait shop closest to the seashore. "When you're young, you can tolerate a lot of spice, but as you get older your tastes ought to gravitate toward blander fare." But Margita and Ben still held hands, still spontaneously embraced when they saw each other on the street, and therefore they had managed to perpetuate what was easily the greatest scandal the town had ever seen. Old Mr. Campbell making passes at his seventeen-year-old grandniece was nothing next to the sight of these two aging lovers, her with her widening hips and the gray that had begun to creep like a fog through her curly black hair, and him with his bald spot and his paunch. (This was before the wheelchair honed his torso to near-Olympic proportions.)

The daytime excursions became unfeasible once Ben's legs had lost their independent function. He had to quit his job, and he no longer ventured out between the hours of dawn and dusk. Margita began taking charge of the household. Her first order of business was to make certain that her husband wouldn't be disturbed while he was home alone. She told his buddies that he was suffering from fatigue and that they had hired a holistic healer to attend to him full-time. This story was sufficient to keep them away.

When her friends called, she went so far as to confide that Ben was very ill (although she was carefully vague about the diagnosis), and in return they loyally cooed their sympathy and sent reams of get-well cards. Only her parents remained unconvinced. In the absence of more specific information, their condolences soon gave way to suspicion and concern. They called two or three times a week, testing out theories of abuse or infidelity, each time pleading with her to come home, to let them take care of her the way they did when she was little. And each time a small part of her considered what it would be like to take them up on the offer, to be enveloped in their arms, to eat platefuls of goulash and spaetzel dumplings until she once again became the little girl with the red-ribboned pigtails who slept sweetly in a room with a harvest moon nightlight. But of course she told them "no." She told them she was sorry that she could not explain further. Then she hung up the phone with a sigh.

Margita's garden went untended and was soon overgrown with foxglove. She spent all her extra time taking care of the groceries, the laundry, the daily chores. She called Ben from work to make sure he was okay. She made him dinner and spent hours in the evening applying his medicated creams. There were times when she was so exhausted she caught herself hallucinating. These spells took the form of quick flashes, and each one lasted only a fraction of a second, like a single out-of-place frame spliced into a film. She might see an octopus in the stuffed-leather chair, or a dove rising from her husband's head. She might see a green-skinned child who would then vanish into the living room wall. She began to feel unanchored from reality. At night, when Ben wheeled himself to the kitchen for a glass of water, Margita often awoke in terror, believing that what she heard was the sound of thunder against the linoleum, the beginnings of a squall that would sweep away the rafters.

Toward the end, of course, even the seaside trips had to be curtailed, as it became too painful for Ben to transfer his blistered body from the wheelchair to the car. He was forced to take up semipermanent residence in the bathtub, buoyed up on a creamy lake of moisturizer. Oddly, the only thing that did improve over the course of his illness was his voice. He had always had a strong, perfunctory baritone, but as his symptoms progressed it had sweetened and become more resonant. Within the reflective acoustics of the bathroom he sounded like an angel. It was as if the malady, having already claimed so much of him as its own, was determined to give him something in return.

THEY MADE NO CHANGE TO THEIR ROUTINE ON THAT final night. They curled up in the armchair, sipped their wine, and watched their favorite stargazer show on PBS. At midnight they retired to the bedroom, where Margita tried her best to stay awake so that she might enjoy a few extra hours of conversation with her husband. But her physical weariness soon got the better of her; within half an hour she had given over to the looming crush of slumber. Ben experienced no such struggle. He had become accustomed to bouts of insomnia over the past months, and anyway his legs were throbbing too badly to permit anything like genuine repose. Instead, he stroked his wife's hair. He folded his hand over the ridged peaks of her spine and reimagined her body as a planet, complete with a warm-glowing core and continental drift. The ears turned into bottomless sinkholes. The ass was a rounded dune with a cleft at its center. The circulatory system was transformed into a network of rivers, and the pubis became an alluvial fan. He watched this landscape rise and fall for the remainder of the night, watched her sandstone feet twitch fitfully as she dreamed.

He wished that he'd been able to give her a child. Something to remember him by.

Early in the morning she wheeled him out to the car. He strained momentarily, lifting himself out of the chair, but his upper body strength was such that he was able to grasp the doorframe with his free hand and maneuver himself onto the front seat with little difficulty. Still, he couldn't help grimacing in pain as his naked legs came into contact with the vinyl. "Sorry, babe," murmured Margita as she placed the old army blanket across his lap. She then began to fold up the wheelchair for storage in the trunk.

"I'm not going to need that," Ben pointed out.

"Yeah, well, it's in case you change your mind."

She said it with a smile, but the bleary-red eyes told the truth. She had been crying since before the alarm went off. (At exactly five forty-five, when she was still asleep and snoring, Ben had witnessed a pair of translucent pearls taking shape at the edge of her eyelids; these eventually broke into rivulets and formed a matching snail-track on each cheek.)

The sun began to crest the horizon as they drove, casting deep veils of red and orange and yellow across the pinioned clouds. It also backlit the car in such a way that its inhabitants assumed the radiant aspect of saints.

"Cassiopeia," Margita prompted finally.

"Reticulum."

"Fornax."

"Corona Borealis."

"Damn show-off."

He laughed and gave her a mischievous wink. They fell silent for the remainder of the drive, which did not take as long as either of them hoped.

When they arrived at the coast, Margita helped him out of the car, helped him out of his faded cotton night-shirt. (On impulse she fastened it to the antenna like an impromptu flag.) They were parked on a high em-bankment, and the sea to the west was still caught up in the gray shadows of predawn. Its surface was silvery; it glistened with light from the low-hanging moon. Slowly, she led him down the winding path to the shore, then out across the beach toward the water. With every step his melded legs kicked up little plumes of sand. They had just reached the tide line, with its wet, ragged edge and its nightly array of seashells set out like an offering, when he motioned for her to stop.

She peered at him curiously. "You don't want to go?"

He replied in a soft voice that was barely above a whisper. "Of course I don't want to go," he said. "I'd stay here with you forever if I could. But the gods seem to have decreed otherwise, and we don't want to get struck by lightning or turned into bulls or anything. Right? Just give me a minute and I'll be ready. For some reason my nerves are giving me hell."

She clasped him so tightly then that her fingernails drew crescents of blood on his shoulder and arms. But he didn't complain. They stood like this for an indeterminate time, two bodies furiously yoked, hearts held together by a filament of will. Their backs were turned against the red-plumed sky and the liquid beyond.

"Okay," he announced finally.

She nodded, and they started out again.

"Remember when we went to the caves, Margita?" he asked as they waded into the breakers, him leaning his weight against her small frame until it was deep enough for him to swim comfortably. "Do you?"

She was shivering. Although her wool shirt and pants were keeping her somewhat insulated in the water, the cold was seeping in from every side, penetrating her flesh as if it were parchment and limning the hidden contours of her muscles. She was aware of them as separate entities—deltoid, bicep, trapezius—each one a solitary strip of meat draped around bone. "Of course, babe," she assured him. "How could I forget?"

Three months into their relationship they had taken a sudden, impulsive trip to see Oregon Caves National Monument. It was midautumn, and the roads had been made slick from the previous day's rain. She remembered how the trees formed a dense canopy overhead, as if claiming ownership of the human realm, remembered those deciduous beacons of ruby and yellow, fiery markers that tumbled like flares and attached themselves to the asphalt below. When she and Ben had reached the caves, they had made a novice effort at spelunking. Neither had any experience. What they did have was the careless bravery of the smitten, two helmets with mounted halogen lamps, and a bag full of glow sticks that they left behind like bread crumbs. As they made their way through the dark passages, they saw ceilings made of marble from the Pleisto-cene epoch. They saw soda-straw stalactites, moonmilk, gypsum flowers, animal fossils, and a wall that looked like it was composed of clusters of petrified bananas. They saw cave fish, also, and Margita had found herself rambling on about the evolution of the eye, how it had developed from a simple photosensitive membrane to the complex globe we know today. The air around them had been moist and smelled of clay, like the begin-nings of the world. This had been a revelation to her. She had never been particularly adventurous when it came to sex, but with these primitive odors saturating her nostrils she had found her bravery and pinned her boyfriend to the wall, removing his cock from its denim chrysalis and awkwardly mounting him.

It was this experience she was thinking of as she opened her arms and felt him surge away from her, this she held onto with that final splash, as something resembling a fin flicked in the air for just a moment and then disappeared beneath the waves. It scattered the moon's reflection into a thousand coruscating particles,

like luminaria in a floating grotto, and though her limbs
began to propel her back toward the brightening shore,
in her mind they were making love again, would always
be making love, lurching into rapture like drunkards,
and setting phosphorescent fires to light their way.

THE ANGEL APPEARING TO CORRINE

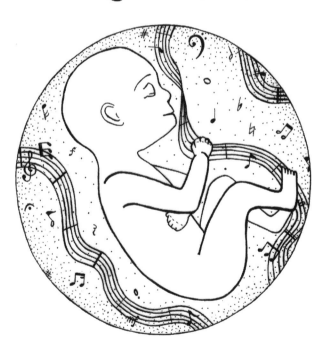

IT BEGINS IN A DRINKING ESTABLISHMENT, AS SUCH THINGS OFTEN DO.

A young woman enters a bar that is unfamiliar to her. Mysterious forces have led her there. While inside, she is visited by a magnificent apparition, and when she emerges it is with far more than she bargained for.

CORRINE DUNNE IS, FIRST AND FOREMOST, A MUSICAL creature. She is forever analyzing the sounds of the city and placing them into their proper orchestral category: woodwind, strings, brass, or percussion. She mentally charts the birdsongs while walking through Central Park. She hears spoken language as a sequence of duplets and triplets, and she often fails to register the substance of people's remarks because she is too busy following the rhythm of their words. She cannot help it. Music is always a presence for her, smoldering within her back like a pair of vestigial wings. It draws her ever upward into strange and airy spheres, where everyday items are made to reveal their hidden selves. A flight of stairs is really an octave. A stack of radial tires is an arpeggiated chord. Freckles and other stray pigments are simply notes that have gone rogue, having slipped off the framework of staff and away from the governance of clefs and measures.

You could say that Corrine is attuned to the harmonic drift of things.

Naturally, there are times when she views this talent as more of a curse. While riding the subway, for example, she cannot keep herself from conducting to whatever song is currently stuck in her head, be it Afrobeat or medieval chanson. There she will stand, with her head held high and her pallid arms outstretched, her hands tracing sail-shapes over the stale air. Down, left, right, up. Down, left, right, up, as if summoning each of the four winds. She knows that people must think she is deranged—God knows Alice did—but what can she do? This is how it has always been.

There is one other thing. This woman is not our newest incarnation of Mozart. She is not a modern ultragenius saddled with a creative gift so powerful it threatens to crush in on her at every second, pulverizing bone and tissue alike with its demiurgic force. No, the truth is poor Corrine cannot compose music to save her life.

She is merely a listener.

ON THE MORNING IN QUESTION, CORRINE WAKES UP thinking of Samuel Barber's "Adagio for Strings." Even in the best of times this piece is a tearjerker. Now, with the breakup looming large in her memory and the collateral loss of the Other Thing that might have been, the piece makes her feel as if she were being embalmed, as if her skin were being plastered over with melancholy, with a dreamy, slow-motion despair. She considers calling in sick, but of course she doesn't do it. Instead, she showers, pulls on a silk blouse and a skirt, places a thin band over her auburn hair and heads for work, doing her best to ignore the siren songs of the Penn Station cellists.

Thus far, nothing out of the ordinary has occurred.

At the office, Corrine is all efficiency. She attacks her keyboard with furious fingers, filling in data forms as fast as she can scan the relevant reports. That is not to say that the music has gone from her. The copier beside her desk is flanked by repeat signs, and the ringing phone emits a cloud of hemidemisemiquavers. When Liam, the office manager, loses his train of thought halfway through a tedious motivational homily, a fermata materializes in the space above his head. (To Corrine, the fermata appears as a holy neon corona, like those of the martyred saints in Byzantine iconography.)

At last, it is her three o'clock break. Corrine exits the office with the intention of visiting her favorite gyro vendor. As she is crossing the street, several things happen at once.

The sky is darkened by a solitary cloud.

A construction worker whistles.

A diseased pigeon falls to earth, just as an FTD

delivery man drops an armful of roses onto the sidewalk in front of her.

A taxicab backfires, and the sound resonates in her ears like timpani.

She is aware of all these things independently; it is as if time is slowing down for her, urging her to take notice of her surroundings, beguiling her into the discovery of some intended place or object. And that is when she hears it—far off at first, and soft, like a succession of tertiary or even quaternary echoes. It is a melody in fragments, and it seems to be issuing from the direction of the Lower East Side.

Here it comes now, sweeping between vertiginous giants of steel and cement. It is moving among the kinetic hordes, glancing off of smooth obsidian walls on its way to find her. The thread of its magic arcs through time and space. It passes over segments of freshly poured asphalt, past graffiti poems and laundrettes and kosher delis and tourists gazing at maps, and wends its way through labyrinths of scaffolding, which stand like recovered whale bones against the buildings. It flows irresistibly toward her in short jewel-like bursts, an audible trail of bread crumbs, and like a child in a fairy tale she is bound by destiny to follow it.

ALICE HAS BEEN GONE FOR THREE WEEKS, AND AL-ready it has gotten so bad that Corrine is contemplating going to Mass again. She feels fearful at night and, during the day, utterly lacking in direction, like a planet that has come unmoored from its sun. With the exception of her job, her life seems to have moved beyond her capacity for control. The little things, in particular, have become impossible to rein in: the hamper is brimming over with clothing; the bathroom tiles are mildewing by the second; and the dust has coalesced into a protective lamina over the end tables. As if that were not enough, the unwashed dishes have all but taken over the kitchen. They have transformed the place into a veritable cave—their malign forms creeping out of the many-chambered cupboard, surging across glossy countertops and accreting like stalagmites on the throw rug.

There is not even room for her to stand—so expansive is her grief.

The breakup occurred over what could only be called creative differences. Alice had made her feelings on the subject known from the beginning, but Corrine had not been able to let it go. Put simply, she had wanted a baby. She had wished for it with all her being, with a great green part of herself that longed to envelop the world. Already, she knew, she carried its imprint within her molecules—her own cantus firmus—and in moments of concentration she attempted to tease out the likely details of its appearance, from its cherubic silhouette to its peach-gossamer hair. She envisaged the baby as a presence within the ether, nestled like a pearl in a mollusk. There it waited, incandescent in its perfection. A susurrus was its only breath, and yet Corrine sometimes thought she could hear its cry while she was showering, or drying her hair, or running the vacuum. She would stop what she was doing when this happened, straining to discern those infant whimpers before they receded back into the firmament.

"Where are you hiding, little one?" she would ask the empty air. "Show me how to find you."

Alice, meanwhile, would be rolling her eyes. "Stop with the charade, honey-pie. This is just like the time you left those sperm bank brochures on the nightstand for me to find."

Alice had been unhappy. That much was clear. She came home late every night, often blind-ass drunk, and there was a good chance that on at least some of these occasions she was fooling around with her ex-girlfriend. There was no question that their life together had become a net of sorts. They were caught in a cycle of ostinatos, doomed to repeat the same conversations, the same sexual games, the same petty bickerings over and over again. Doomed to attend the same book readings by the same erudite lesbian authors, and doomed to make the same curried rice every Tuesday night until the end of time. But Corrine did not mind the lack of novelty in their lives. She loved Alice, and with every repetition, every ritual, she felt that love more deeply, like a river-path limned into stone. Had Alice ever really loved her back? She doubted it. If the woman was enamored of anything, it was probably the idea of Corrine, the idea of her extraordinary condition and the manifestations thereof. She must have loved the vision of herself as witnessed through Corrine's eyes, loved the notion of herself as muse, just as she loved to hear Corrine's descriptions of her many attributes: the exquisite tablature of her dark skin, the ears that resembled bass clefs, the fierce brown eyes that took command of the surrounding spaces with the beatific assurance of whole notes. And really, is there anything so unusual about this kind of arrangement? For men and women of uncommon perception, admirers, groupies, and hangers-on have never been in short supply. But where these others can sustain the enchantment by rendering the lover in portrait or in song, Corrine had no such finished product, no such illusion of immortality to offer her partners. Her small eccentricities amounted to nothing. Aside from her synesthesia, she was almost hopelessly mundane. She worked for an insurance company. She had a habit of avoiding eye contact with strangers. She was plain, even. All of these were facts that Alice was more than happy to point out on their last meeting, angrily and with considerable bile, as if she believed herself to have been duped somehow.

"Besides," she said, "you're already married to your ovaries. You're the worst thing in the world, honey-pie. You're a cliché."

And Corrine had to admit that it was true.

So it was that their spark passed from the earth. Alice departed in a pillar of flame, and the baby they might have had vanished into the residual smoke.

THE LOWER EAST SIDE IS THE BACKDROP AGAINST which our miracle is set. Over the past decade the area has undergone a revival, so that exclusive nightclubs and trendy boutiques now coexist with payday loan stores and homeless shelters. Sooty parking garages moon and sigh over freshly restored Federalist-style brick buildings. There are topless clubs, gallery clubs, leather clubs, rock clubs, billiards clubs, cocktail clubs, both low- and high-rent comedy clubs, even a bur-lesque club. There is a movie house that used to be a boxing venue. There is a tenement museum, and there are hundreds of examples of the genuine article all around it. (It is said that nineteenth-century chimeras lurk behind those eerie, punched-out windows.)

Corrine walks through all this as if in a trance, one ear held to the pulse of the air, until at last she arrives at a shabby little saloon she has never seen before.

She notices first the strange quality of the light. The burnished afternoon sun is pouring in through the open door—drowsy, mysterious, and bathing the floor-boards with the lush hue of infinity. The beam is like the cross-section of a comet trail. Within its span she can see millions upon millions of dust motes, and her first thought is that the music in this place must have somehow taken physical form, that each particle she observes is actually the reified remnant of a note, the word made flesh, so to speak.

Soon her eyes adjust and she is able to take in the details of the eclectic decor. The bar, for starters, is nothing more than a battered, antediluvian pickup truck with a wooden counter jutting out from it. There are Christmas lights strung along the counter, and the barstools are covered with faux cowhide. A full-sized statue of Johnny Cash stands guard outside the men's and women's bathrooms. Along the wall there are a number of shallow niches, arch-shaped depressions that are lined with shells and pieces of sea glass. Each one contains a treasure: the beads Janis Joplin wore to Woodstock; an eye patch from one of Bowie's Ziggy Stardust costumes; a promotional photo signed by the original members of Pink Floyd; Tom Petty's sunglasses; Freddie Mercury's leather cuff; Beck's harmonica; and half the lyrics to "Jane Says" scribbled on a truck stop diner menu.

Under other circumstances, Corrine might have the presence of mind to wonder if these artifacts are authentic, and if so, whether the bar owner could have possibly come by them in an honest fashion. But such suspicions do not even enter her thoughts at the moment.

She is already spellbound by the music.

CORRINE HAS ALWAYS BEEN PARTIAL TO OPERA, BUT truthfully she cannot reject any music that reaches her ears. It is as if she is lacking an immune system; the most bromidic pop song has no difficulty worming its way into her consciousness, disturbing her dreams and polluting her bloodstream with its infectious rhythms. As for the truly great artists, she has always been helpless before their power. She is consumed by Coltrane. Bruised by Brubeck. Ravaged by the Ramones. Bewitched by the Beatles. Devastated by Dylan and humbled by Hendrix.

So when this new music coils around her, creeping up her trunk and braceleting her arms with its double helix chords, she is entirely at its mercy. She does not know how to resist.

The band is an alt-country ensemble, comprised of two guitarists (one playing the pedal-steel variety), a drummer, a keyboardist (who is also the singer), and an upright bass player. The second guitarist has a banjo slung over his back, ready to switch at a moment's notice. The drummer has a spare washboard and spoons. A sixth person is playing a saw, a "found" instrument that has moved beyond its practical origins and is now busy casting fearsome tendrils of vibrato throughout the room. The singer wears a floral cotton dress. She has a voice like seduction itself, like a soul that has been broken over too many sorrows.

Corrine has never heard anything like this music. It

is tragic in texture, full of beauty and lamentation and full-bore eroticism. A distant landscape seems to issue from the woman's mouth as she sings. The walls of the bar fall away. The truck dissolves into a sea of pixels, which flicker for a moment in the empty air before blinking out. (She thinks: *this must be how it looks when brain cells are short-circuiting*.) All at once, Corrine finds herself standing on a kudzu-choked portico, besieged by the twin terrors of heat and mosquitoes. Beads of perspiration begin to form between her breasts. Her silk blouse cannot cool her. The humidity in the air is intrusive, ubiquitous. It is not like in the city, where atmospheric moisture ebbs and flows like the tide. She can smell the red clay soil and taste the iron oxide on her tongue. She sees cypress trees that are thick with ghosts. She hears her own name caught in the throat of a sandhill crane. Finally, a caesura occurs in which she is aware of nothing but a profound sense of rapture, like being warmed by the sun for the very first time, like those early afternoons with Alice, when hands became crude instruments and grace notes floated up from her lover's shimmering, sweat-soaked skin.

In the midst of this ecstasy she finds these thoughts within herself:

(1) that she is highly favored;

(2) that whatever she produces shall also be highly favored;

(3) that she should not be fearful but rejoice.

WHEN SHE WAS JUST A LITTLE GIRL IN THE BRONX, her parents regularly took her to Sunday morning Mass. She can still see the tableau plain as day: her father on her left, with his wire-rimmed spectacles and his navy blue suit and his fastidious ex-Lutheran beard, who always passed her candy after the Eucharist; and her mother on the right, whose flaming hair belied the seriousness of the occasion, who wore low-cut dresses even in winter, who clasped her daughter's hand extra tightly because she knew there would be no other children, who was passionate and intemperate and Catholic through and through. As for the contents of the service, Corrine remembers little that was not chanted or sung. In her mind the choral elements were not merely ornamental; they were the very substance of the worship experience itself. Together, they formed a kind of organism, whose ephemeral life began and ended within the span of the Mass.

First there was Kyrie, the wondrous birth, then Gloria, when Mary's heart liquefied and leaked out through her tender eyes, then Credo, which was the rough-hewn spine of the created world, then Sanctus, the roiling spirit. Next it was Benedictus, the path of senescence, and finally Agnus Dei, the incanted death, the alchemical process through which the soul of that great thing passed through stained glass panes and ascended to heaven in a curl of divine smoke. These choruses were strung one after the other, like rosary beads. But within their compass there was something ancient, something that was far older than Catholicism in particular or Christianity in general, something that predated even the Romans (from whom the magic and the mystery were pilfered). It was the same force that had haunted the earliest peoples of the earth, nesting in their blood and enabling them to see the mark of divinity on animal skins; to ponder the miracle of consciousness; to walk upright one moment and find rhythm the next.

Corrine has not been to Mass since she was eighteen years old. Her parents had just been killed by a drunk driver, and after watching the dotted half-notes of Fauré's Requiem float up from the orchestra at the funeral (like cartoon goldfish with X's over their eyes), Corrine decided there was too much sadness in that place to return. That was the first reason. The other reason was that she remembered all too well the humiliation of the confessional, how she had felt compelled to rattle off the same transgressions week after week, the same unwholesome feelings about which she could do nothing but burn with shame. Her friend Claire had had an embarrassing crush on Jesus. But Corrine's sin was even worse than that.

She had been in love with Mary.

Mary of the tender heart and the Seven Sorrows.

Mary of the miracles.

And now here she is, and a similar miracle is occurring within her own body. Something minuscule is taking root. A leitmotif of sorts, a single theme that has carried across the ages to settle within her womb.

Her face becomes radiant. Her veins pulse. Her nostrils are filled with a sickly-sweet fragrance. A thin, pearly fluid begins to leak from her breasts, causing a pair of dark moons to form on her blouse. But Corrine is too far gone to care about such things. You see, she can finally hear the baby again. She can hear its plaintive cry, like a silvery filament woven into the band's sultry harmonies. It is so close now she can almost touch it, can almost pluck it from the air and hold it to her chest. This is not just any child, after all. It is her dream child. It belongs to her already—the heart outside her heart.

Corrine's limbs have been loosened by a surfeit of bliss. As she reels alone in the center of that shabby bar, the other patrons can only gaze on her in wonder. Even they, the mid-day drunks, can see that something singular has happened here. Even they can see that she is blessed.

So begins the slow, nine-month crescendo.

ppp, pp, and *p.*

Everyone in her division is baffled by the change in their coworker. Each morning Corrine sweeps into the office on a piece of sky, encased in a cocoon of light. They can hardly bear to look upon her, so luminous is her aspect. It is obvious that there is a secret tucked away like a jewel inside her. She has not become an extrovert exactly, but she is far more outgoing and pleasant to everyone than before. She smiles at Liam when turning in her weekly reports. She sometimes joins her colleagues for drinks after work (although she insists on ordering ginger ale, rather than liquor or beer). She no longer talks about Alice.

mp, mf, and *f.*

The urine test at the clinic comes up negative. The doctor tells her that the thing swelling in her belly is a tumor and encourages her to schedule a CT scan as soon as possible. But Corrine only laughs; she knows what she is carrying, and she explains as much. It is a baby that will be born of sound. Perhaps it will have no material substance whatsoever, and will instead be comprised entirely of sonic waves. Rather than measuring pounds and inches, the hospital staff will be forced to catalog the frequency and wavelength of the infant. In lieu of hair, there will be gently thrumming cilia, and euphonious oscillations in place of eyes. Ungraspable fingers will exert pressure on the nurses' palms. And of course, there will be an invisible heart keeping tempo through it all, beating out the primitive percussion of systole and diastole.

She knows she is right several nights later, when she feels the quickening in her belly. It is like flashes of lightning on a far-off horizon. Muted but unmistakable. It is as if that second heart is coming drowsily to life, groaning and stretching and unfurling its thick-muscled wings.

ff, fff, and finally, *ffff.*

At the end of the ninth month Corrine feels a warm gush of fluid between her legs. For a moment she can only marvel at this development. How extraordinary, she thinks, that liquid should play such a pervasive part in the advancement of organisms throughout history, from the earliest microbes bubbling in the deep sea, to her own gravid body, whose amniotic sac is the modern analog of those primeval trenches. How extraordinary, that water should be the idée fixe from which all biological variations flow.

She dials 9-1-1, and within half an hour is being wheeled into an ambulance by a couple of paramedics with dyed-black hair who are listening to Radiohead. "At least you have taste," she remarks, before passing out. Next, rolling down the hospital hallway on a stretcher, she sees the lights lined up above her like a sequence of half rests, like beacons glittering on a landing strip, guiding her to her destination. Once again, the air seems to be thick with a sweet fragrance—a heady, cleansing aroma, redolent of frankincense, copal, styrax, myrrh. She is convinced that someone is walking behind her with a censer. She can almost hear the thurifer's footfalls, can almost see the wide parabolas of his arm movements as he casts brumes of white smoke in her wake.

She can also hear the catechism of the nurses' questions—when did she last eat? does she have any allergies? has she had trouble urinating lately?—but she is unable to answer.

THE PAIN IS NOT EVEN PAIN ANYMORE. IT HAS BONDED with the music that is already encoded in every atom of her body. It is raw jubilation and piercing hope. It is exquisite euphoria. It is acute, unyielding gratitude. And somewhere within the diapason of these sensations, which have begun to swirl around her like a crude electrical field, Corrine can once again hear the auguries of the country singer. Can once again hear that broken-soul voice and the counterpoint of her own heart.

In the operating room things begin to accelerate. All her life, it seems, has been building up to these moments. The love, the loss, the synesthesia; the piano lessons with her mother, the days at the park with her father; the rapturous Sunday morning Masses and the tears they elicited; the first time she heard the White Stripes on the radio, the first taste of alcohol, the first time she felt the warm crush of another girl's lips against her mouth; the tedium of high school, college, and a seemingly endless string of data entry jobs; the trip to London, when she rode the Tube by herself for hours at a time; the street fair where she met Alice;

even the pillars of dirty dishes that nearly took over the kitchen when she was still bewildered and drowning in grief. Each experience vibrating in different keys, each one an aural placeholder for a vast realm of memory.

She is opened up with a scalpel. Everything converges upon a single point, the tiny blossoming seed at the center of the universe. And that's when it finally happens—her dream emerges from its otherworldly grotto. Trembling, panting, laughing, and weeping (although by now her lower half has been fully anesthetized), Corrine brings forth her magnum opus.

The doctors can only stand back in awe.

No one can think of a single thing to say.

Now the miracles begin to come thick and fast. All at once, an impossible breeze curls across the floor, agitating the hems of the surgical gowns so that they rise and fall like ocean billows. The air becomes suddenly, unaccountably warm. The smell of incense is so powerful that the staff is becoming light-headed. And that is not all. Within moments everyone in the room makes a phenomenal discovery—they are able to decrypt radio signals. Somehow, doctors and patient alike have gained the ability to interpret these ambient waves, to separate and examine each rarefied thread, tuning into whichever frequency they prefer. For the lead doctor this means choosing Latin jazz, the music of his birth country. The interns beside him choose industrial, hip hop, and psychobilly, respectively. One of the nurses singles out "Rhapsody in Blue," while another opts for the Tom Waits song that was playing the day she and her husband renewed their marital vows. Corrine, not surprisingly, settles on the final aria from *Tristan und Isolde*. The beautiful, heart-shattering "Liebestod." The one where the lover dies.

The team does their best to remain professional. They keep carrying out their prescribed duties—irrigating the cavity, applying sutures, sponging off the blood—but it is with a practiced, mechanical hand. In truth they are already far away. They are swimming in circles of fifths. They are exploring pentatonic caverns. They are scaling lofty glissandos. When they finally finish with Corrine they go tumbling into the hallways with tears streaming from their eyes and their tongues full of song, baffling the crowd that has begun to gather in the waiting room. "What the hell is wrong with that doctor?" "Is she drunk or something?" But soon the phenomenon spreads like fire among the patients, transmitting epizootically from person to person, prisming out from a central point like charges from a Tesla coil.

Everyone who hears it becomes feverish with joy.

Everyone who hears it is blessed.

Back on the operating table, Corrine smiles. Her auburn hair is matted with sweat. Her body feels strangely absent, as if she is separating from the core of herself. The quality of the light in the room begins to shift, becoming crepuscular and slightly unreal.

Isolde is singing.

Isolde is singing.

AND SO THERE IT GOES, THE TRUE CHILD OF HER SOUL. What began in an unswept bar has now come to glorious fruition. Flowing and chromatic, it is like a passage out of Philip Glass. It mingles with Corrine's own faltering voice, harmonizing with her, surpassing her the way children are meant to do, departing into a bright day where it is already making its mark. There it will burn and shimmer and thrive, illuminating everything in its path until some point far, far into the future, until long past her own death, or Liam's, or lovely Alice's, or the doctor's, or that of her priest back in the Bronx. Beyond the building and leveling of skyscrapers and the writing of symphonies. Beyond the flourishing and withering of civilizations, when the Lower East Side has finally succumbed to blue-shadowed entropy; when everyone who has ever been born, from Cleopatra to her beloved parents, has long since sent their carbon ghosts out into the world to be recycled as leaves and fungi and the corded sinews of other living creatures; when the diversified drone of existence tapers back to a single sweet note; when the earth is once again robed with green and all of our philosophical murmurings are just a dream that troubles the sleep of animals; when the child's magnificent oneiric life has at last spun itself out and it comes to rest at the place of its own coda.

But it is a million years till then.

In the meantime we of the human race have once again had our salvation renewed (or, conversely, received our stay of execution). Once again we live in a state of grace, watched over by our most venerated saints, our Debussys, our Björks, our Wyclef Jeans, our Ella Fitzgeralds, our Jeff Buckleys, our Sondheims, even our Johnny Rottens. For who has not come to believe, while listening to any of these, that he was a storm-petrel plucking fish from the glistening shallows?

That he was, in fact, walking on water?

LIMBS

It was early morning in the valley. A gauzy sheet of stars still lay across the sky, swept high against that distended bowl, but as the eye moved eastward those fiery pinpoints began to fade, began to dissolve into the auroral glow that banded the horizon. Red-tailed hawks were beginning to stir in their aeries, their thoughts rapt with visions of corpulent prey. Lacewings flapped drowsily along the steep-banked hills. And at the bottom of the valley, beside the path that circumscribed the lemon grove, a mother's world was coming apart, her famous composure buckling beneath the latest confession of her five-year-old daughter.

"You shouldn't have done it," Alejandra said when the girl had finished. "Now we'll have to leave this place. We'll have to find another grove to work in."

As the woman spoke she lifted lightly scarred fingers to her neck, withdrew the bandanna that was draped there, and tied it in a triangle over skeins of coal-black hair. Her dark eyes were luminous, flashing portents.

"But it wasn't my fault!" cried the girl. "He dared me!"

"How many times have I told you, Marquita? If people find out about us, we won't be safe here."

The girl wiped away a tear, nodding miserably. She

jammed a single hand into the pocket of her denim jumper.

"Where is it now?" demanded her mother. "Does Luis have it?"

"I don't know . . . I dropped it when I was running. I'm sorry, Mama."

"All right, we'll take a look."

And so together they scoured the grass-robed hill that stood beside the grove, saving their closest scrutiny for the western slope, where the youngest children liked to gather. They were searching for something that would appear to be a length of copper among the green. Something that at first glance might be mistaken for a hank of rolled leather, or a larger-than-average gopher snake. But in the half-light, they could make out very little. Shapes merely glided, split into segments, and then vanished again among the monochromatic shadows on the ground. Soon the sky grew brighter, and they were afforded a brief window of visibility until the sun hit the morning fog and rendered the hillside all but opaque. Only then, with a glittering haze coalescing around her ankles, did Alejandra admit defeat. She parked her daughter behind a row of sagebrush and left to find Hector.

As she crossed the rocky path, Alejandra scanned the area for signs of trouble. Clouds of ladybugs rose up from the bull thistles, thick as locusts in a swarm, but so far there were no disturbances of the human variety. The workers seemed to be fully occupied with their picking.

Perhaps the boy has not yet told what he has seen, she thought. *Or perhaps he did, and he was not believed.*

BY THE TIME HECTOR'S WIFE APPROACHED, THE *baño* beside the tree was nearly full. His chestnut skin was already lacquered with sweat. His cheeks shone, his brawny forearms sported a high gloss, and there was a slick triangle apparent where he had begun to unbutton his chambray shirt.

"Howdy, ma'am," he said to her in English, and the other workers laughed.

"Would you come here for a minute?"

Hector stopped picking and wiped his brow with his sleeve. He gazed down at his wife. Fifteen years ago they had met on a strawberry farm outside Ensenada, and he had known from the first moment he saw her that he wanted to marry her. He thought about how fervently he had pursued her, and how Alejandra, who was well aware of her many charms, had delighted in placing obstacles in his path. Now, three children and countless hours later, Alejandra seemed lovelier to him than ever. He had never been able to remain faithful to a woman until she came along. And yet, with her it was easy. Her oval face inserted itself into his every thought. Her body was sinuous like smoke. He dreamed about her black hair falling in curtains around him, about the knife-curve of her shadow, about her secret mutant magic. Coyly, he raised an eyebrow at her. From time to time they had been known to slip off into the brush for a midday tryst. But Alejandra, catching the seed of his desire as it wafted toward her, gave him an impatient look that said, 'Not today.'

He sighed and climbed down from the ladder. "Well, what happened?"

"It's Marquita . . ." she said in a low voice. And although myriad hands continued to move through the rustling boughs, the level of conversation in the grove fell off noticeably. She could sense them all straining to hear, could almost see their ears rotating like satellite dishes toward them. "Come with me," she muttered, leading the way.

They were well clear of the grove when she felt it was safe to speak up. "We have to get out," she said, her long legs taking prodigious strides that his shorter ones could barely match. "That boy Luis said she couldn't do anything special, so she proved him wrong."

"What are you saying?" Hector asked, feeling suddenly queasy. "Are you saying she took her arm off again?"

WHEN THEY REACHED MARQUITA, MOODILY KICKING at rocks behind the sage, the arm was already partway regrown. Alejandra felt her anger begin to subside.

Here it was, the giant genetic arrow pointing from herself to her daughter.

No difference between them would ever be as significant as this single thing they had in common.

And of course she could not deny a certain tenderness associated with the regenerative process—it was like watching a fetus take shape in the womb.

First there was the stub. Soft. Vulnerable. No more than a tiny, fleshy mound emerging from the socket. Next, the arm began to lengthen, forming a loose chrysalis that would soon be populated by cords of blood, muscle, and bone. It swung to and fro as it grew, circling like a pendulum, before abruptly curving to the left and solidifying into the crook of an elbow. At this point the growth of the skeletal structure sometimes outpaced that of the epidermis. It was not unusual to catch a glimpse of ultrawhite, gleaming like a unit of plumber's pipe, as the radius and the ulna shot out on their twin trajectories away from the body. Eventually, the arm flattened out to form a hand, and after that came the fingers, which sprouted like plumage, like a rosary of twigs pushing out from the palm. Sinews stretched taut across metacarpals. Fingernails grew like gibbous moons. Blood vessels branched out and opened for business. The entire transformation took several hours to complete, and even then you did not have a perfect double for the lost appendage. The new skin was too smooth, too pink in color. It didn't yet match the rest of the body.

"It hurts, Mama," the girl whimpered.

"I know," said Alejandra, scooping her up. "I know it hurts."

Hector looked thoughtful. "Let's just consider our options for a second. I mean, do we really need to leave? We don't know yet how everyone's going to react."

"Yes, we do. Remember what happened last year? When they found little Manolo?"

Last September a new worker had appeared in their ranks, a Caucasian man, which was not in itself unusual, although from the beginning the other workers had found him to be peculiar. He rarely spoke to anyone, ate all his meals alone in his trailer, and showed no interest in becoming part of the community. One night they had all been gathered for dinner, the adults singing songs and drinking mescal, while the children spiraled out from the cook fires like the arms of a great galaxy, reemerging just long enough to swipe Jarritos or tamales from the steamer pot. As such, it was several hours before someone noticed that six-year-old Manolo was missing. Rafael was the one who found the boy on the far side of the grove the next morning, catatonic, his legs mangled by dozens of cuts with a machete. They managed to get him to the hospital in time to save his life; however, he would never again walk without the aid of crutches. He and his mother had been seized by border agents immediately following his discharge. As for the perpetrator, the men of the camp had tracked him down a mere two miles away from the grove, where he was sleeping like a baby under a willow tree.

"Do you remember what they did to him?"

"Of course."

Alejandra looked as if she were about to set forth the gruesome details of the episode anyway, but a quick glance at Marquita's fearful face caused her to think better of it. "And that was a white man, Hector. A *white* man. No one would even come looking for us."

"He was also an outsider. Look, Alejandra, these are good people. We've watched each other's kids, shared our food and our water, worked extra when someone was sick and the foreman was going to fire them for not making quota . . ."

"Doesn't matter."

"Why not? Remember, you're not in that village by the ocean anymore. People here are more enlightened."

"In my experience, people are never that enlightened."

Hector watched his wife pull their daughter closer against her shoulder. Her eyes were ablaze, and her slender arms formed a cross around the girl's body, as if shielding it from threats both natural and supernatural. "Okay," he said at last. "Okay. If we start packing up now, maybe we can get out before anything happens."

WHEN ALEJANDRA HAD AGREED TO MARRY HECTOR, it was under the condition that he perform a Herculean task of some sort at their wedding, as well as every year on their anniversary. The task was his choice, she had said, but it had to be spectacular, and upon its completion it was not to be repeated. Each task must be unique: a wonder all its own. It was an absurd and extravagant demand, one she had made of all her suitors, and thus far it had been effective in repelling every interested party from her door. But Hector had readily agreed to her terms, had even angered her by feigning nonchalance at the prospect of fulfilling them.

Thus, on the day of their wedding, brimming with bravado and eager to demonstrate his mettle, he had prepared to jump a twenty-foot ravine with his vintage Norton motorcycle, his prized possession, which was just like the one Che Guevara used to ride. Though he felt this feat was likely to get him killed, the anticipation of it had only served to increase his ardor. Certainly, his brothers believed him to be mad. His widowed mother fell at his feet, begging him to reconsider. No woman was worth such a risk, she cried. But Hector was singularly aflame with love. He would not be dissuaded from his grand gesture. He had spent the past few days packing the dirt just so, shaping the contours as if for his own mounded grave, creating a ramp that he hoped would carry him across the precipice, or at least a good portion of it. He had elected not to make a practice run. Somehow, that seemed a betrayal of the greater objective.

And so with the wedding party lined up across the

ravine like a necklace of gleaming teeth, he had gunned the bike, producing an accusatory growl from the engine, and launched himself up that incline of dirt as if it were the only means of ascending to heaven, as indeed he felt it was. The wheels lifted. The earth fell away as if it were nothing, as if it had never truly existed. For an eternity he simply hung there, caught like a bird between drafts of air, in essence weightless, an astronaut on an unplanned EVA. A haze of unreality enveloped him. The dusty hills resembled sheets of grooved cardboard, while overhead the sun glinted like a tinfoil star. But there was his lovely new wife below, the beacon drawing him back to earth, and as he fixed his eyes upon her he saw that the aura of indifference she had worked so hard to maintain during their time together had melted away entirely from her visage. She beamed up at him, her expression adoring, proud, and so, so hopeful.

He managed to reach the far side of the ravine, but the bike lost traction upon landing, skidding on its side for about fifteen feet and dragging poor Hector with it. As a result he had a nasty road rash up the length of his left thigh. The pain merely glanced off him, however; it was unable to penetrate the cloud of his euphoria. At the party that night, with Alejandra draped rapturously across his lap, his leg in bandages, he boasted to everyone that his was the consummate battle scar.

After this first display and at Alejandra's explicit

urging, his feats had become more ceremonial in nature. Her heart required no further bloodshed. Instead, he spelled her name in candles outside their trailer, or gathered the mariachi to serenade her, or drove all the way to Juarez to buy her a blouse she had once admired. He thought with pleasure how his wife was like one of those clams hidden among the rocks on the shore. To all appearances she was a rock herself: formidable and unyielding. No one but him knew the surprising softness within. With each child her shell had edged open a bit further, its angle increasing by increments, so that he was often amazed by a glimpse of some hidden pearl of thought or the dispensation of a previously undisclosed memory. But of course her biggest secret was the one he had known all along, ever since that golden day at the ravine: she loved him just as much as he loved her.

THE BOYS CAME WANDERING OVER THEN, SENSING A family crisis. "What's going on?" demanded Aureo, who had recently turned thirteen and felt he was owed adult explanations.

"A boy saw your sister take her arm off."

The middle child, Argento, seemed unimpressed by this news. "Well, maybe no one will believe him," he suggested.

Alejandra shook her head. "They will if he has the arm with him. It's not like it could be mistaken for anything else, like a Halloween prop. And it's too clean to have been taken from a corpse. It won't start decomposing for days."

"What if we just hang out here and wait for Quita's arm to regrow? There wouldn't be any proof then."

"No good. Even one person knowing about us is too many. We don't want to take any chances."

Aureo glowered at his sister. "I knew this would happen," he snapped. "I knew this was all too good to be true, and one of you'd do something to screw it up. I've got a girlfriend, you know."

"Yes, we *know*," sighed Argento.

Hector pointed a finger at his oldest son. "That's enough. Your sister already feels bad about what happened. Tell her you're sorry."

"The hell I will," barked Aureo. "I've got to get started packing! We're in such a goddamn hurry, right?" And with that, he took off in the direction of the trailer, leaving the father with no option but to plunge into the grass after him. Hector's fists were clenched as he walked, and shimmering clouds of profanity issued from his lips.

"There they go," muttered Alejandra in disgust. "My two *caballeros*."

In truth, she knew that Aureo had had a rough time of it over the past few years. It had not been easy for any of them to live such a transient existence, but it had been especially difficult for one who had just experienced puberty and was, day by day, testing out

versions of the man he wanted to be. Just when he
had most needed to feel anchored, there were rumors
of a raid and the family had had to set sail once again,
abandoning the last encampment in favor of the lemon
grove where they currently found themselves. Aureo
had been furious. He would not speak to her or Hector
for weeks. His one consolation upon finding himself in
this new locale was that he had been permitted to ride
his father's motorcycle in the evenings, racing along the
rolling hills with the wind sublimating his lean body,
stripping away particles of grief and fear and doubt so
that only his essential self remained. But that ended, too,
when Argento nearly died of pneumonia and they'd
had to sell the bike to pay for his hospital stay. And
now this. Yes, he had found Nieve, and Alejandra was
grateful for her, for the deep-sea glimmers of happiness that passed across her son's face when he thought
no one was looking, but every day she had wanted to
warn him that it couldn't last. There would always be
another sacrifice.

She worried far less about Argento, who had few
attachments and an unassailable inner world. When
he was small, he had had a veritable army of imaginary
friends, so many she could never keep them straight,
and these he deployed like warriors whenever he was
sad or frightened or simply going about his daily business. He talked to them constantly, so that at times
Alejandra felt she could almost see them, seeded within

a fold of sunlight, swarming like bees around his tiny frame, like miniature gods, each with its own protective function. Then there was Marquita. Poor Marquita, who would tender a lifetime of secrets for a single moment of affection. Alejandra sighed. She had always thought they would have enough money by now to buy their own place, a little stucco house with violet sage and a rock garden, but of course things hadn't worked out that way.

Argento took hold of his sister's remaining hand. "Don't worry about it, Quita. He can always get another girlfriend. Anyway this one smelled weird . . . did you ever notice? Like skunk cabbage."

But the little girl didn't seem to hear him. She was crying in earnest now, lifting her head only occasionally from the dampened spot on her mother's shoulder. "Mama," she sputtered at last. "Why are we like this?"

Alejandra considered the question carefully. She thought back to the time before she met Hector, when she was propositioned by the overseer of the guava farm she'd been working on. He had told her she had no right to refuse him, had even threatened to have her arrested, but when he grabbed her arm to try to force her to the ground she was able to wrench away from him, leaving the appendage fixed within his grip like a misshapen bat. By the time he had recovered his senses she was long gone. That was the beauty of the thing. The effect produced was not unlike that of a magician disappearing within a puff of smoke. It disoriented. It stripped the brain of its assumptions. It caused a crisis of faith in the workings of the natural world.

Gently, she ran her hand over her daughter's blackbird hair. "So that when we're caught, it's because we *want* to be caught."

BACK AT THE TRAILER, THE FAMILY WAS LOADING UP the trunk of the lime green Charger. They didn't have much, but it was amazing how their belongings seemed to swell and multiply within that space, like an unwelcome miracle, so that soon the children began to bicker about what items warranted inclusion in their exodus.

In the absence of Hector's intervention—he was in his own world, poring over faded photos from their wedding—Alejandra began issuing instructions. "Grab a few knives and forks, leave the rest. Take the portraits from their frames and pack them inside your schoolbooks. Leave the furniture and the lamps. Take two rolls of toilet paper and a couple of bath towels. Take the pillows. Take all the cans of vegetables except the beans. Leave the fridge alone; all of that will just spoil anyway. Oh, and each of you may take up to three personal belongings, but they have to be small enough to fit on your lap. Now hurry!"

The family got to work. Their hands flew across shelves, walls, counter tops. Fingers that were made agile from fruit picking were now culling the artifacts of their lives. And just as each piece of fruit they picked was a hole punched in the air, delineating the sprawling, organic shape of the tree, each object they chose was a point on a map of their memories, a guide to the identities they hoped to preserve.

"I'm not going," announced Aureo finally. "I'm a man now, and I can make decisions for myself. This is where I want to be."

"It's not a question of where you want to be, it's where it's safe for you to be."

"What do you think's going to happen? We'll be lynched like a couple of whores in Juarez?"

Alejandra dropped the pan she was holding. It clattered dully to the floor, and for a moment she simply stood there, frozen, her head bent over the countertops in an attitude of desperate prayer. Perspiration gleamed like rosary beads on the back of her neck. Aureo took a small step toward his mother, believing that she was about to cry, but before he could apologize she whirled and slapped him hard across the face.

The boy's hand rose to his cheek in disbelief. In the entirety of his life, his mother had never struck him. His father sometimes did, when he was particularly mouthy, but never Alejandra. She was the sensible one. The one who showed restraint when everyone else was showing their teeth. The protector. "That's it," he said finally. "Nice knowing you all."

Just then Marquita began to shout. "Somebody's coming!"

The rest of the family instantly crowded around her at the window. There, in the lot outside the trailer, was Luis's father, a burly man named Juan-Carlos. He wore a leather eye patch over his right eye, having been partially blinded by a rogue branch several years earlier. In his hand was a small pistol.

"Dammit," muttered Hector. "I'll go talk to him. You boys get yourselves in the car and get ready to go. Marquita, stay in the trailer for now."

He trotted down the stairs, looking admirably casual as the boys slipped out on either side of him. "Hey, Juan-Carlos," he said. "How's it going?"

The man eyed the car and the open trunk. "What's going on here?" he demanded. "Where you folks heading off to all of a sudden?"

"Puerto Angel. My mother's health is failing, and we're going back to stay with her for a while. Something I can do for you?"

"Yeah," said Juan-Carlos through gritted teeth. "You can tell me what the hell's going on with your kid. My boy comes to me and says she pulled some kind of trick on him?"

"Sounds about right. She's been playing pranks on the family all week. What'd she do now?"

"Took her arm right out of its socket is what he said. Just yanked a little bit on the wrist and off it came, clean as a whistle. No blood or anything. Showed it to me, too, and I got to tell you it looks pretty real.

He's awfully upset . . . thinks your girl's some kind of monster, I guess."

Hector laughed. "You should see her when we try to give her a bath. Turns into a regular Chupacabra! Anyway, I'm sorry she played a prank on Luis. I'll speak to her about it."

Juan-Carlos scratched one leg with his gun hand and leaned toward the open door of the trailer. "Mind if I take a look?"

"At what?"

"Your daughter."

"It was just a magic trick. She probably had her arm tucked inside her sleeve."

"Just the same I'd like to check it out. Won't you indulge an old man's superstitious nature?"

"I really don't have time for this, Juan-Carlos."

"Oh, it won't take any time at all."

Before he had a chance to reply, Hector looked up to see three more workers approaching from the grove. Close behind them was another group of three. And they kept coming. They were stepping out from the trees like zombies in a horror film, the sun flaring up behind them, dimming their features to a uniform gray. Hector scanned the faces in the gathering crowd. There was Victor, who had taken Aureo and Argento to the beach more times than he could remember. There was Cesar, who often delighted Marquita with his dramatic guitar renditions of *Tengo una Muñequita*. There was

Jorge, who had been writing passionate love letters to Alejandra since his own wife died the previous year. (As a gesture of respect, he always permitted Hector to read them first.) And then there was Rafael. His temperament had undergone a radical shift following the incident with poor Manolo; once good-natured to a fault, he was now prone to suspicion and fits of anger. He was also Nieve's father, and in the past months he had grown increasingly concerned about her relationship with Aureo, though as far as Hector knew it had not progressed beyond a few stolen kisses. No doubt Rafael would be pleased to see them gone, but otherwise the assembled group was comprised of people Hector considered to be friends. People he knew well. People he trusted.

Soon, even little Luis came to stand beside his father. He was brandishing the purloined arm, holding it before him like a torch.

ALEJANDRA HAD JUST TURNED NINE WHEN THE VIL-lagers discovered what she could do. In the beginning they had treated her as a saint, even worshiped her for her strange ability, which they believed was a sign that the Blessed Virgin had at last taken a special interest in their village. Her neighbors cast wreaths of marigolds at her feet when she walked through town. They incorporated her name into their favorite hymns. They built grottoes for her on the rocky shore, adorned with elaborate mosaics that glistened like jewels in the salt spray. They brought her wooden idols carved to resemble stags and salamanders. (Each one of these was painted a vibrant blue, so that when she held one in her hands, she found it easy to imagine that she was looking at a piece of the firmament, a star-cloaked relic fallen to earth.) The villagers even lavished her with food—fish and honey and pitchers of warm goat's milk—and for a while she and her widowed mother lived very comfortably off these tokens of her presumed sainthood.

Then things began to go wrong. There was a season of drought, and many of the livestock died. The red snapper all but vanished from the coastal waters. By the time a neighbor's infant son was mauled by a rabid coyote, people had begun to harbor suspicions that the little girl was not the Blessed Virgin's emissary at all, but in fact a sorceress whose black arts were the true cause of their calamities. On the night of the next full moon, they came for her. Her mother had just enough time to conceal her beneath the floorboards in the kitchen before a mob of villagers came crashing in, ropes and fishing implements in hand.

In that cubbyhole, with her cheek pressed against her grandfather's secret cash box, Alejandra had blacked out from fear. She had awakened the next morning to find her mother's limp body hanging from the doorframe, the word "bruja" etched into her lovely forehead.

Now, as she surveyed the proceedings from the

trailer window, it was all coming back to her. She felt again the cold metal of the cash box against her skin, the paralyzing terror, the sensation of looking upward from her own coffin, even the texture of her mother's hair between her fingers when she stood on that high stool, cutting the body down.

She felt, also, Marquita's heart beating wild against her chest. But there was nowhere to hide her, no loose floorboards. She found herself wishing that she could make a refuge of her own flesh, that she could locate one of those gulfs that exist between atoms and fold the girl into it. The child had already come through the portal of her body once; why could she not, just temporarily, slip back inside? What was the use of Alejandra's distinctive anatomy if she could not even do this small thing for her daughter? She did know they couldn't keep hiding in the trailer like this. The longer Hector tried to stall the workers, the more likely it was that tempers would flare and an incident would occur. And so she did the only thing she could. She shifted Marquita on her hip so that the half-limb was not apparent from the front and, genuflecting, stepped outside.

"Somebody declare a holiday?" she asked with smile. "What's everyone doing here? Oh, hello there, Jorge. You're looking very handsome today."

Jorge merely blushed and looked at his feet.

Now that she was outside she had a clearer view of the situation. There were twenty or so workers forming a ragged arc around the trailer. Some of them held weapons, some didn't. She was relieved to see that in spite of all his bluster, Aureo had obeyed his father's command and ushered his younger brother into the car. The older boy sat peering warily out the window, his fingers splayed frog-like against the glass.

"We just want to take a look at your daughter," said Juan-Carlos apologetically.

"I'm afraid she's not feeling well today, Juan-Carlos. Got a bit of a fever. I think it'll be better when we get on the road and she gets some wind on her face."

"Oh . . . certainly. No doubt it will." He cleared his throat, at a loss for how to proceed.

Rafael came forward then. "Look, we just want to know what's going on. The boy here's got an arm that he says came from your daughter . . ."

"Marquita."

"Yes, and you can see why that sounds kind of fishy to everybody." He took the arm from Luis and began to examine it, running his rough-hewn fingers lightly along the surface. Hector bristled. "Looks real enough to me," Rafael reported finally. "Soft and smooth, and just the right size for a child her age. Even got those little downy hairs on it. Question is, where'd it come from? Exactly what are you folks involved in?"

"Involved in? What could we possibly be involved in?"

"I have no idea. Some kind of child slavery ring, maybe. Who the hell knows?"

Alejandra was incredulous. "We're here fifteen hours a day picking lemons, same as you. When would we have time to operate a child slavery ring?"

"Well then maybe you just go around chopping off little girls' arms for fun."

"Look, Rafael," said Hector, whose voice had lowered to a menacing growl. "There's no crime here, no mutilated children. Just a *cabrón* with no brains making accusations."

Alejandra shot Hector a furious look, one of those lightning-quick admonitions couples share when they've known each other so long that communication is reduced to a series of chemical signals between bodies.

Rafael started forward, but Alejandra interceded, holding up her elegant hand in a placating gesture. "All right!" she shouted. "All right. Just cool it, everyone." She waited for the commotion to die down before continuing. "I'll tell you all the truth." Here, she required a deep breath. *Am I really going to do this?* "Marquita has a very rare condition . . ."

There was a guffaw from the back row.

"It's true! Her condition is so rare they don't even have a name for it."

"What is it?" Jorge prodded softly. "Is she going to be all right?"

Alejandra shot him a grateful look. "Yes, she'll be fine. Her condition isn't terminal, and most of the time it doesn't cause her any pain. Look, I'm sure you've all heard about animals that can regrow their body parts?

Like starfish and lizards and such? Well . . . that's what Marquita does. If the situation requires it, she can detach one of her arms and leave it behind. Later it'll grow back, good as new. See for yourself."

Slowly, apprehensively, she turned her daughter's body toward the assembled crowd.

The reaction was immediate. The workers cried out with shock and outrage and pity. Faces went slack, or contorted into baroque expressions of revulsion. Victor looked like he might vomit. Cesar was forced to steady himself against a fellow worker. Jorge removed his St. Louis Cardinals cap and pressed it to his chest, as if Alejandra had just told them that the girl was terminal after all. And then there was little Luis, who was thoroughly fascinated by this most recent revelation. Evading his father's grasp, he bolted forward to inspect his friend's truncated arm, which by then had produced not only a perfectly pink elbow but also four inches of virgin flesh beyond. It described circles as it grew, bobbing in the air like a damaged wing. It looked hopelessly fragile. But Marquita held it out for him to touch, and so he did so, his fingers twitching with delight.

"It's awesome," he whispered.

"I told you," she said.

Alejandra turned back to the onlookers. "I'm sorry we didn't tell you all before, but we were just trying to protect our baby girl. I'm sure you can understand."

There was a bewildered silence, and then Juan-Carlos

finally spoke up. "Well I'll be damned." He quickly slipped the pistol back into the waist of his jeans, seeming abashed by its presence. "Ma'am, all I can do is beg your pardon for the intrusion. I don't know how things got so out of hand. After Manolo last year . . . well, I guess we're all just a little on edge."

"Quita's an angel," added Cesar. "Of course we want her to be safe."

Jorge, his hat blooming like a bright wound against his chest, looked positively stricken. "We've made a terrible mistake. I see that now."

One by one the men came up to apologize, beginning with Victor, who had recovered from his momentary nausea. They shook Hector's hand and tipped their hats to Alejandra. She made certain to greet each one warmly, assuring them that all was forgiven.

Only Rafael seemed unpersuaded. "I want to see it," he said.

"See what?"

"A demonstration."

"No! There will be no demonstration. My daughter is not some kind of carnival attraction."

Marquita was suddenly afraid. "I don't want to, Mama."

"No one's going to make you," Alejandra replied. "And no one's going to hurt you, either. Right?" She cast her fierce gaze around the semicircle, daring them to respond. "Right?" she asked again.

One by one, the workers murmured their assent.

Behind them, in the sun-drenched grove, the lemons were shining like particles of light against a sylvan canopy. Their rinds had lately turned, and they were now the deep, saturated yellow that could only be achieved when the fruit was mature and ready for sale. Alejandra wondered obliquely whether any fruit in the world was as beautiful as a fully ripened lemon. Its hue was like something out of a fever dream. And it grew only more intense as the day wore on, so that by late afternoon you often had to let your eyes go out of focus to keep from being mesmerized by it. Even in the twilight, the lemons retained traces of their luster. The women would be cooking menudo over a stone-ringed fire while the men rolled tobacco and still the lemons could be seen, winking like portals among the darkened limbs, their rinds slivered through with shards of amber. Hector, who was an animist at heart, liked to say that he could hear them calling to him as he curled into bed, a kind of organic siren song.

I have been too hasty, she thought. *We may not have to leave after all.*

The atmosphere seemed to have cooled a good twenty degrees since the exchange a few moments earlier. Even Rafael was nodding his agreement, albeit somewhat grudgingly. To calm him further, Alejandra placed her fine-boned hand on his shoulder. "*You* have a daughter, Rafael. We just want what's best for them, don't we?"

But mentioning Nieve was a mistake. Across the

man's weathered face appeared a shadow—quick, flitting, like a dusky wing occluding the sun. And then he made a sudden grab for Alejandra's throat.

This caught her entirely by surprise. She managed to jerk away at the last second, escaping his grasp, but in doing so she lost her footing, and both she and the child fell back onto the gravel. Hector cried out with rage. He lurched forward at his wife's assailant. Soon, he was battering Rafael with his massive fists, while the faithful Jorge rushed over to protect Alejandra from further attacks. Aureo, too, sprung into action. He made a beeline for his little sister, who had fallen against her mother and was unhurt, and swept her up in his arms, even as the parking lot transformed into a hail of flying fists. Little by little he inched through the fray, carrying her over his head like a trophy, until at last he reached the Charger and placed her beside her brother in the back seat. It was only then that the rigid wire of her body finally relaxed, with the noise dampened and her dolls set across her lap and Argento trilling out all her favorite *corridos* in his gentle, high-pitched voice.

The men, meanwhile, were doing their best to restrain Rafael. They grabbed at his legs. They applied headlocks. They generally attempted every *luchador*'s trick they could think of. But in his madness he seemed to have developed superhuman strength; he was brushing them off like nettlesome insects. And then, in the chaos of the moment, he managed to seize the gun from Juan-Carlos. He began to swing it wildly around the circle, a compass needle seeking north. Hector surged forward, hoping to disarm him. But it was too late. The trigger was already being pulled.

Aureo had just enough time to catch his father as he fell. He hooked his slender, adolescent arms around the top of the man's bulky chest and, keeping his limbs loose, his body pliable, accepted the surplus weight onto himself. He became an immovable object. A steadfast fixture. He swayed like a birch tree, but he did not topple.

As soon as he felt certain of his balance, Aureo hurriedly maneuvered his father into the passenger seat of the car. He tried not to look at the ring in the gravel where Hector had stood. Still, he was aware that it had begun to blossom a rich red, as if the fluid were boiling up from the heart of the earth rather than sluicing onto it from above, as if what had just happened was so unfathomable that gravity itself had been suspended and reversed as a result. For a simple leg wound, it was truly a prodigious amount of blood. "Let's go," he said grimly to his mother.

Jorge had been escorting Alejandra to the car when the shot went off, and her willowy frame was still frozen into a stiff contrapposto by the rear of the vehicle— her head half-turned, her gaze trapped in a nightmare of memory. But at the sound of her son's voice, her thoughts snapped back to the present. She gave Jorge a quick peck on the cheek, slammed the trunk, and slipped neatly behind the steering wheel.

It was then that Rafael broke free of the mob again. He charged toward the vehicle, even as its engine came growling to life, and though the gun had been reclaimed he was not about to let its absence deter him. He moved faster than they had ever seen him, much faster than the workers who were attempting to give chase. To those watching it seemed that his rage had taken physical form; it stretched ahead of him as he ran, curling outward in dusky plumes, eating through the air like acid and smoothing the way for his passage. And he very nearly achieved his objective. His gnarled hands were already grasping, clawing through the driver's-side window when Alejandra put in play the final ace up her sleeve. She disengaged her left arm and lobbed it like a bomb at his chest.

"There's your demonstration," she said.

And then they peeled out, a faded streak of green along the chalky road where the bumps lay in patterns like ribs, like hash marks plotting the distance from some giant heart. The road began a precipitous climb, curved slightly, then dropped again, so that it was only a matter of minutes before Rafael disappeared from view. Aureo, who had been watching out the back window, breathed a deep sigh of relief. He pronounced their escape a success. And yet, as the air grew cooler and the scent of ripe lemons rolled down after them like a cloud, Alejandra could not shake the feeling that the grove was even now extending its tentacles in pursuit of them, that it was not about to let them go without a fight. In the mirrors, the retreating landscape could be seen warping and rippling in the midday sun. How long, she wondered, before a tide of wayward leaves came surging over the hill, before the brume driven by her long-eluded fate began lapping against the tires and breaking with botanical fury upon the burned-out roof?

By the time they were halfway to town, Hector had mostly succeeded in stanching the flow of blood. He had fashioned a crude tourniquet from his belt, secured it around his upper thigh, and then gripped the end of the strip tightly in his hand, as if it were a leash he was afraid to let go of. "It's not all that bad," he said, trying not to grimace. "We shouldn't risk going to the hospital."

"A bullet taken anywhere on the body can be fatal," recited Aureo.

"That's true," Alejandra agreed. "Anyway, I know a place where they don't ask for ID. We'll be in and out of there in no time at all."

"You don't get in and out with a bullet wound," Hector laughed. But his wife didn't respond. She was already retreating from him, vanishing behind her silken curtain of strategy and survival. Instead of pressing her further, he turned his attention to the back seat and regarded his children. Argento was gazing contentedly out the window. Aureo, having come through for the family when they most needed him, appeared to be slipping back into his role of angst-ridden teenager. He was slumped over in his seat, looking sullen. And between them, Marquita was busy playing with three brightly painted Catrina dolls—three of a set of four.

"Where's the other sister, Quita?" Hector asked.

"Mama said we could only bring three things, so I left Miss Purple."

"Oh," he said. "I'm sorry, honey."

Hector thought of the abandoned figurine, elegant in her violet gown and flower-trimmed hat, standing a lonely vigil at the window of the trailer. He wondered how long she would be allowed to remain at her post. Most likely she would be scavenged by one of the other families for their own children, but if not, how long would she last? Fifty years? A hundred? There was no fabric to rot; she was carved entirely from dried clay. And she was already a skeleton. It was almost as if she had come into the world knowing that she would one day be left behind, as if she had carved herself into that condition of gaunt loveliness as a shield against this inevitable parting.

"Guess we'll have to go to another school now," said Argento, who had started flipping through a stack of anime-themed trading cards.

Aureo turned to his brother in disbelief. "We're going to be deported, you moron."

"Either way we'll be at a different school."

Hector had to grin at this. Argento may not have

inherited his mother's regenerative abilities, but what he did have was an evolutionary knack for tolerating change, for riding out storms with equanimity and a sense of detachment that might be called grace.

"No one's getting deported," said Alejandra gruffly. "And I don't want to hear anybody mention that again. Understood?" This admonishment was greeted with silence. To Hector she said: "I'm sorry. I know you loved that place."

"It's just a place," he replied with a shrug. A slight tightening of her jaw told him she knew this was a lie. "Anyway, I'm hoping this gets me off the hook for this year's anniversary feat." He let out a little barking laugh.

Suddenly, his body began to seize. His brain submerged beneath a wave of blinding pain, and when he at last he resurfaced, he was aware of Alejandra peering intently at him, her mask of mild concern punctured through with terror. She placed her one remaining hand in his lap, cupping his manhood briefly before taking the wheel again. "Hold on, Papi," she whispered.

Hector closed his eyes and nodded. Her touch had aroused his memory of their first lovemaking, and so he found himself contemplating anew how her sinewy legs had wrapped like vines around his trunk, and how his heart had then fallen to earth, flaming, ready to bring forth the seed of planets. Was it really so terrible that they were leaving his beloved grove behind, the same way they had left the last grove and Mexico before that? The family would surely survive. They would anchor themselves to a fresh patch of ground, a fresh universe if need be, and if that one didn't suffice then they would just have to find another one that did. Universes were legion, after all. Infinite as limbs.

Marquita's voice piped up. "Mama . . . what if we don't make it to the hospital in time?"

"We'll make it," Alejandra said firmly, her features once again stoic as a sphinx. "We'll make it."

EDNA, FILLED WITH LIGHT

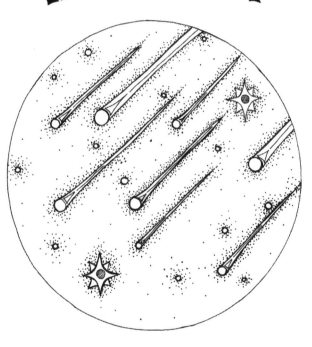

IT WAS DECEMBER OF HER EIGHTIETH YEAR WHEN THE METEORS CAME TO EDNA.

They were great, sublime things that arrived in the night like providence, if that were something she believed in. Perhaps the dimensions of her weathered face were the clarion call that drew them forth. Each crease, each furrow, manifesting an echo of their home worlds, singing to them where a smoother face might have repelled. They had been waiting. All her life they had been waiting. She knew that their hearts were rock, but oh, their roughened husks—how they could be made to smolder. It was in the quick of the fire that they came alive at last, no longer coy, now brazen and fairly flashing with meaning. *My scientist's brain has fallen to decay*, she thought. *I have at last attained the romanticism of the old.* But the sense of meaning persisted. And like revelations falling upon one another the meteors began to increase in scope, in magnitude, in intensity. Somewhere beyond Earth's atmosphere they bred like rabbits, the richness of the planet an aphrodisiac too powerful to resist. Soon they were so numerous that they blocked out the nighttime sky, and then that of the day.

But it was not this way at first.
At first there was only one.

SHE HAD BEEN ON THE BACK PORCH, NURSING A MUG of hot tea when she saw it.

Edna must have seen thousands in her lifetime, and yet the sight of this particular meteor, casting its silvery reel across the eastern Kansas sky, produced in her a visceral jolt, a sense of clarity that was like awakening after a long illness. In that instant she was five years old again, having stolen into the garden to observe a predicted meteor shower. She was wickedly barefoot, her toes digging tiny graves in her mother's flower-bed, while her yellow hair lashed in the wind and her heart pounded to life—she had never known she had a heart till then—and the Perseids blazed in a glorious band above her.

For as long as she could remember, Edna had watched for falling stars. Through poplar branches and the glint of car windows her eyes sought them out, those quicksilver threads, their arrival always un-expected, seemingly serendipitous. When her mother, an avid reader of *Nature*, explained that these were wayward hunks of rock and metal drifting through space, she found that she cherished them all the more. She set aside her notion of falling stars as mere wish-dispensers and instead began to dream of them in graphic scientific detail. Their physiognomies were wondrous to her, etched and scored as they were from collisions with other celestial objects. She imagined sliding her fingers over their dimpled surfaces, pressing them into the folds of her skin, even ingesting them (in tiny pieces, of course). She pored over what few photographs she could find (NASA would not be created until she was in her twenties) and as a teenager pinned the best ones to her wall the way her friends put up posters of Gary Cooper or Van Johnson. Something about their condition spoke to her. Even as she grew older and embraced microbiology, the small in opposition to the large, her love of meteors remained tucked away inside her, a vestigial organ lined with stardust.

Truly, the meteors seemed to offer wisdom for every epoch of her life. As a young adult, they served as a reminder that she did not belong solely to the duskier regions of the earth, to the gas stations, supermarkets, law offices. She was a complex organism dwelling on a living planet, itself part of a vast and ever-shifting universe. After the accident, and then later, in middle age, they offered an example of the dangers inherent in such a universe. Scattered across those reaches were suns that metastasized into red giants and, like scorned lovers, laid waste to their planetary wards. There were galaxies that crashed into one another in slow motion. Rogue comets and asteroids that came hurtling through deep space, blind and ravenous for contact. Even black holes, which Luc had once called the psychopaths of the cosmos. (He was the only one she could talk to about such things—Everett was primarily interested in the terrestrial: the lab they shared, the medical artwork he did as a hobby, Edna herself.) And in older age, around the time she and Everett and Luc had retired, they whispered to her that life was short, that what was yearned for today should not be postponed until tomorrow. Collectively, they formed the unified theory of a life. Her flesh aged and her personality drifted like an itinerant landmass, but at her core she was always that same little girl in the garden, aflame with bliss at the beauty of the stars.

She pulled Everett's old Cowichan sweater tightly around her. Outwardly, there was nothing to distinguish this new meteor from others of its kind. It was remarkable only in the way that they all were, like beautiful, lost children. Perhaps its duration was a trifle longer than usual, but in her euphoric frame of mind she did not give the matter much thought. Indeed, as she watched the meteor describe its arc overhead for one, two, almost three whole seconds, she was aware only of a vicarious heat settling over her bones and the sanded-down cogs of her joints, conquering, for an hour at least, the arthritis that had for so long been in residence there.

Edna scanned the sky for another hour, but no further visitants appeared. It didn't matter. She climbed into bed in a daze, drawing up the covers as if to bring this pleasant episode to a close, hoping it might provide a bulwark against the inevitable nightmares.

NEW YORK CITY, 1959. THE LIGHTS SEEMED TO BE everywhere at once. Red, white, blue. The colors of patriotism, of mom and apple pie. They appeared in wild, pulsing arcs that slid across her cornea like a finger on a map. She could not get a fix on them. They were disembodied somehow, dissociated from their points of origin, as if they were not native to her world at all but were seeping through from some adjacent reality. Their endless convolutions maddened her. The sirens, too, which chipped at her consciousness like an axe, like a lobotomy in progress, so that she found herself wishing they would just hurry up and get the job done. Rubies of blood curled from her lip, their iron sting detonating upon her tongue. The front seat of the taxi was daubed with red, as were the armrests, the windows, the roof. Blood was the network that held the human body together, but now it seemed that it had been holding the car together as well. It was as if the vehicle had been merely an exoskeleton, a placeholder for some membranous being that had already vacated the premises, lifting from the wreckage like a liberated soul.

There was another sound, too, forming a ragged wall behind the sirens and the shouts of first responders, and once she heard it, she could not hear anything else.

It dwarfed all lesser noises, put their insignificance in crude perspective. It was the sound of steel buckling and scraping against itself. She was certain she would lose her mind before her body could be extricated from the debris.

Within the tiny pocket of space and time she inhabited, the world seemed to be ending, shrinking to the size of a pebble.

Then she felt Luc's hands on hers, and the world burst open again.

EDNA OBSERVED TWO METEORS THE SECOND NIGHT, mere minutes apart. The third night it was four in quick succession. When the subsequent night brought sixteen, she felt a flutter of trepidation. Still, it was probably nothing. Wasn't the human brain always teasing out patterns where there were none? She thought of the great ancient civilizations, the Chinese and the Greeks, yoking the stars into the shapes of gods and heroes. Overlaying meaning onto an uncommunicative sky.

She tried to go about her life as if nothing had changed. She had her meals at the usual time, took her customary three-mile morning walk, perused the astronomy magazines at the library in the afternoon, and chatted with the other retired researchers at the coffee shop in the evening.

But the more she tried to put the meteor problem out of her mind, the more it vexed her. It had somehow

set its roots in her, becoming the idée fixe that permeated her every thought and movement. The meteors
insinuated themselves into the cornices and doorframes
she passed. They peeked out from between sidewalk
segments and filled in the gaps in her conversations.
They were visible in the domed curve of a lettuce leaf,
the airy pages of a magazine, a child's footprints in the
snow. They were encoded in the winter wind, and in
the crude language of gooseflesh. There was no escape
from them. Indeed, Edna reflected that her preoccupation with the meteors was not unlike the experience of
being in love, with its general elevation of the senses,
and, more troublingly, the accompanying certainty that
something rare and numinous lay just beyond the mar-
gins of her skin, that she had only to move through
space to touch it.

THE ACCIDENT HAPPENED DURING AN IMMUNOLOGY
conference in New York, a scant four years after she and
Everett were married. Everett had stayed home to work
on a project, and rather than face the subway alone,
Edna elected to take a taxi each day to and from the
convention center. The first few days passed without incident. On the third evening, after a late workshop, she
climbed into a cab with a wealthy-looking businessman.
He tipped his hat to her; she nodded politely. They
promptly forgot each other. But snow had fallen heavily
throughout the day, and after only a few minutes, the

vehicle hit a patch of black ice and lost control. They skidded for about twenty feet—long enough for Edna to conclude with irrational certainty that they were slipping off the edge of the planet—before crashing headlong into a brick edifice abutting an alley. The driver, a friendly Irishman, was killed on impact.

Four of Luc's ribs were broken, as well as his left arm. Edna had multiple lacerations in the vicinity of her ear and midsection, and her leg had been pierced through with a scrap of jagged metal, narrowly missing the femoral artery. It seemed to take hours for the emergency crew to pry off the damaged doors. And so they waited, unable to turn their eyes from the specter of the dead man. There was a shocking vulnerability to his body in this state. He could not arrange himself to look better, could do nothing to avoid further mutilation or indignity, and it was with this anatomical candor that he bound them, his wool coat flapping in the wind like a priest's cassock, his hair a ruddy halo clotted with blood. It was only when they loaded her onto the gurney that Edna realized her tweed skirt had been torn up to the thigh. But by then it was too late to cover herself.

EDNA FOUND HERSELF IN A STATE OF INCREASING AGI-tation as she awaited the next night's meteor shower. To calm her nerves following dinner, she went out to retrieve her mail. She was unsurprised to see Arthur, her next-door neighbor, standing vigil at his own mailbox. Arthur had been married twice, a widower two times over, and she gathered that he was one of those men who could only truly thrive if there was a woman in the house to look after him. Edna herself had no intention of getting married again, especially if she was expected to fulfill the role of caretaker. Still, Arthur was handsome for his age, and clever (a former lawyer), and she liked him well enough. And so she lingered there, chatting amiably, while dusk fell over the street like a tenebrous curtain.

The first of the night's meteors appeared before the sky was fully dark. It hung there for what seemed like an eternity, burning like a white-hot brand, and this time its path was circumscribed by a diffuse smear of light, which radiated far beyond what might have been expected for a meteor of this size. When Edna tried to draw her neighbor's attention to this phenomenon, however, he claimed to see only the usual suspects: Perseus, Cetus, and, of course, Orion. She was irritated by this evasion, but she didn't have time to argue with him. She had to count. She tallied each of the 255 remaining lights, her lips moving as she did so, and by Arthur's silence she began to understand that he had not been lying about the meteors. He genuinely could not see them. He remained a while longer, perhaps holding out hope that her moment of senility would pass, before gathering his mail and shuffling back to his house. Edna suspected he would not wait for her by the mailbox again.

But Arthur's opinion of her was a trivial thing compared with what she'd just discovered. *I can't believe it*, she thought wildly. *It's exponential. That means tomorrow there will be*—she quickly did the figure in her head—*65,536. Incredible.*

Once inside, Edna checked her laptop for any active meteor showers being reported for her area. But there were none of any significance, had not been for months and months. Neither were there any stray satellites whose orbits had decayed, their metal shells plunging unceremoniously toward earth. The International Space Station remained on course; according to NASA's online tracker, it was currently skimming the atmosphere over Africa. What then? Aliens? Some sort of terrorist attack? She could credit the government with the will to conceal such events, but in practice it would be damn near impossible. And of course the fundamental questions remained: why these signal fires or vessels or whatever were visible only to her, and why their appearance followed a specific mathematical progression.

But no, she was making assumptions again. In her research she had seen the truth of Occam's razor borne out too many times to ignore it. The simplest explanation often proved to be the correct one. And in this case, there was one painfully simple explanation.

She had had a stroke.

Edna contemplated the possibility with more sadness than fright. Everett had experienced a stroke some years earlier, leaving the left side of his body partially paralyzed until the day he died. Despite his outward stoicism, she knew it had been devastating for him. And yet, there was no paralysis in her case. She thought about the rest of his symptoms and contrasted them with her own. Her peripheral vision was intact. There were no balance issues to speak of. Range of motion was as expected; her arthritic arms ached as she rotated them, but equally. And her speech was unimpeded. Arthur may have thought she was raving, but there was no doubt that he had understood what she said. Nor did she think it was Alzheimer's; her memory was as sharp as ever, and her symptoms were too specific to be consistent with diffuse cognitive breakdown. A tumor then? The very idea irritated her. She had worked so hard to stay in shape, had endured a lifetime of copious exercise and a disciplined diet. But of course she couldn't stave off bodily deterioration forever. By eliminating some of her potential deaths, say by heart attack or liver failure, she unwittingly opened the door for others. As an immunologist, she should have known this better than anyone.

A tumor was certainly plausible. But then, she had experienced no seizures, no headaches, no sudden bouts of nausea. So what did that leave her with?

And this time as she asked the question, an answer appeared to her, like words upon a clouded mirror.

They are here for me.
The meteors are here for me.

THROUGH SOME GALLANTRY ON THE PART OF THE hospital staff, Edna and Luc were placed in adjoining rooms after surgery. In the first few days, when she was half-mad on morphine, she was able to keep her sanity by tethering her perceptions to the sounds of Luc stirring in the other chamber. His drowsy moans of pain as he shifted in his cot. His comically loud snores. His murmurs to the nurses in which she heard her own name pronounced repeatedly, as if he had forgotten the answer given to him moments earlier: How was she doing? Were her injuries healing well? Could he be taken to see her? But he was forbidden from leaving his bed, just as she was. The shared bathroom began to take on significance as a portal between planets—if only one of them could pass through it, they could be in the other's world.

And then the third night, it happened.

She saw him first as a flicker in the doorway. An out-of-place shadow. Then the bed lamp in the opposite room flared up behind him, and she could just make out the wiry body, the sweat-damp hair, the strong jaw that was like an arrow taking aim at her. His torso was wrapped mummy-tight, his left arm pressed like a broken wing against his chest. She saw that he was waiting for some sort of acknowledgment, and so she answered him with the slightest nod, a gesture so small she could have disclaimed it for the sake of conscience. But of course he understood its meaning well enough. Limping to her bedside, he took in the scope of her injuries, took in also the slender form beneath the hospital gown. (In her febrile state she had cast the blanket aside.) Under such scrutiny, Edna was acutely aware of the unsightly wounds that canvassed her flesh. She was chagrined by their brazen self-evidence, by her body's total lack of shame in advertising its own trauma. Yet there were no signs of revulsion from Luc. Instead, he bent to where her legs lay uncovered, braced himself with his good arm, and then lowered his mouth to the gash just above her right ankle. She felt his tongue dart out, lightly sealing the wound. After a moment he moved on. One by one, his lips attended to each bruise, each laceration, first on one leg then the other, taking his time with the most severe one, with its bright red sutures that zigzagged the length of her left thigh like a child's first yarn project. At its apex, his hair briefly made contact with the hem of her gown. All the breath seemed to depart from her body.

Everett would never have done something like this. This was something new, something heretofore unimagined, and the prospect of Luc continuing both thrilled and terrified her. Already she felt as if she were drowning in sensation. The stars beyond the window pierced her eye. They filled the room, populating the hollows in her bones and temporarily blotting out the driver's contorted face. She became conscious of her body on a microscopic level. She considered her brain, her organs, her endless networks of tissues, in which each cell performed its duties like a stalwart machine, spinning out both pleasure and pain. ("Cell," she remembered, was from the Latin *cella*, for "small room," and indeed her body seemed to have become a sprawling mansion, its teeming chambers crying out for discovery.)

Once Luc had completed his initial circuit, however, he was unable to go on. He clutched at his ribs, whispered an apology, and with his wounded-animal stride, hobbled back to his room. Edna could only lie in her skin and burn.

Edna wasn't willing to accede to the whisper just yet. To rule out optical anomalies, she sought the opinion of an ophthalmologist. She had endured cataracts for years; they were summarily removed. As a result, her vision was clearer and sharper than it had been in ages. The colors alone were a revelation. Brilliant hues seeped back into the world, unmasking the radiance of trees, of faces, of her crimson nail polish and emerald green walking coat. The first sunset she saw was so vivid as to be artificial, like one of those paint-by-numbers portraits you'd find at a thrift shop. She watched its progress with tears that stung her still-inflamed eyes, feeling unmade by the intensity of the display, conscious even of a creeping blush that something so provocative should be viewed by just anyone on the street. And yet, when night fell, she observed that her situation had not materially changed. The meteors were more numerous than ever—a sea of ghost ships breaking against the horizon.

On her follow-up visit, the ophthalmologist, a young man with shoulder-length auburn hair (which was much more vibrant than she had previously thought, like a nighttime fire on the prairie), assured her that her retinas exhibited no signs of a stroke or other catastrophic event. He concluded that the continuation of her symptoms was the product of some sort of neural miscommunication. "The brain is a squirrelly thing," he said affably, as he scribbled some notes in her chart. "Your eyes have been corrected, but your brain may still think there is an obstruction preventing them from seeing properly. These meteors are likely just shadows cast by an unbelieving brain. They will fade in time." He gave her a broad grin and rose from his chair, dismissing her.

Edna stared back at him for a moment. Should she explain her own background in science? Scold him on his ageist and possibly sexist assumptions of her ignorance? There seemed little point. "You're an idiot," she said finally, and gathered up her things. The young man was startled—the smug demeanor dissolved instantly—but he allowed her to go without further comment. It was funny; people always expected old ladies to be nice.

In fact, she *had* been nice in her youth, before the car wreck turned her world upside down. She had made it her mission to be gentle and measured in all situations, and people had done nothing but tread all over her. Many people had been fond of her, but few had respected her. Now, she was cranky and opinionated, and it turned out that people respected that plenty.

The ophthalmologist was right about one thing, though—she did have an unbelieving brain. She was a skeptic by nature, a true scientist, and only believed those things that had been authenticated by experiment and peer review. In the case of the meteors, very little of this methodology was available to her. She had only her own observations, and it was becoming clear that her peers would be unable to corroborate them. All she could do was document the experience for as long as it endured. And so, rather than subject herself to further foolishness from the medical establishment, Edna made her way to the campus observatory to take a closer look at the mystery.

THE FOLLOWING NIGHT SHE AND LUC PICKED UP PRE-cisely where they had left off. And as their broken parts healed, they began to try out other maneuvers, testing themselves among the hulking shadows of medical equipment and the gaudy floral arrangements sent by colleagues, pushing their patchwork bodies even further than the doctors did in physical therapy. They were fearless and inventive, unconcerned with the inevitable pain, for it was bearable, even pleasurable after a point. Moreover, the exertion seemed to have a beneficial effect on the healing process. Everyone said that their recoveries were remarkable.

Things changed somewhat when Everett flew in to be with her. The sympathies of the staff had been with them before—a bit of marital transgression was understandable given the ordeal they'd endured—but there was something unseemly in how they persisted even after the spouse was there to pick up the slack, something tawdry in how they waited, coiled like snakes, counting the minutes until visiting hours were over. The nurses began to sigh while changing her dressings, and mutter under their breaths, and shake their heads, until at last Edna grew exasperated and snapped, "It's not really any of your business, is it?"

Truly, Edna had never pictured herself as the type of woman who would have an affair. And yet being with Luc was so natural she had scarcely felt an ounce of regret over it. It was not only that he was good-looking, though his pale green eyes were certainly capable of impairing anyone's judgment. It was also that he had become her aegis against despair. Since the accident, Edna had noticed the atmosphere thickening unbearably around her. Respiration had become difficult, and her limbs were as heavy as lead bars. But when she was with Luc—when he was inside her, breathing her name—she sensed none of that. She could no longer feel the weight of the dead man, his head lolling back as if to make a breezy remark. Her limbs felt only airiness; they became bright planks in a scaffolding of light.

While Edna spent her days being waited on by Everett, or talking him through his latest research predicament, Luc entertained a full retinue of visitors. He was called on by his bank associates; clients; the three clerks who worked for him and were compelled to conduct business in his absence; Antonia, his secretary, for the same reason; and numerous lovely, unattached women whom she identified as girlfriends. The latter he put off in the practiced fashion of philanderers, charm and flattery intact, yet promising nothing. Often he chatted amiably with Everett while she had her wounds treated, and at this he seemed practiced as well. Whatever he was, he was no stranger to clandestine affairs.

During these endless daylight hours, Edna had a persistent sense of being shipwrecked, of being stranded somewhere wild and uncharted, her body whipped raw by salt winds. Though she carried on full conversations, she felt herself beginning to convolute into the shell of the bed frame. The walls moved in ripples around her. She kept her insights lashed tight against her invertebrate heart. It was only at night, when she and Luc had exhausted themselves with lovemaking, their arms and legs entwined as if to anchor each other to earth, that she at last let go, letting them pour out of her like seawater. She proffered all her stories, sought his in return. She told him about her mother's love of science and learning, her splendid garden, and even her proud resourcefulness during the Depression, how she had taken in the occasional afternoon caller in order to keep the household running. He told her how in 1938, his entrepreneur parents, sensing impending disaster in their native France, had fled to America with their lanky young son, arriving in New York on Luc's twelfth birthday in the midst of a terrible storm. He remembered how the city's vistas had unfolded to an eternity before him, how he saw his brand-new soul etched in the lightning across Central Park. The lovers held back nothing. And they repaid each other by taking the other's perspective seriously, however effusive.

In describing her work, Edna often found herself rhapsodizing the beauty of the small, the way endless worlds were swallowed within one another, like concentric circles on a tree trunk. She catalogued for him the bacteria and parasites found on or within the human body, noting that inside each parasite was a wilderness of even tinier components. ("So if our eyelashes touch," Luc asked in mock horror, "the mites that live on them will jump back and forth between us?" "Absolutely," she grinned. "I'll have some of yours, and you'll have some of mine. It's all very romantic.") She told him also how she loved the atom, although she had loved it a little less after Hiroshima and Nagasaki. Luc, in contrast, loved the large. Banking was only a means to an end for him. He had a catamaran and loved to race it in tournaments, skimming indigo seas with the wind whipping his shaggy hair. He dabbled in Alpine mountaineering. He wanted to get his pilot's license. He had plans to journey to Antarctica in order to re-trace Roald Amundsen's historic path to the South Pole.

"You have to come with me," he said brightly. "We'll be the Bonnie and Clyde of adventurers, raising hell all across the Ross Ice Shelf. And if I ever make you angry, you can make me sleep in a pile with the sled dogs."

She laughed at this. "Oh sure. You'll be warm and I'll die of hypothermia, and the problem will sort itself out."

Above all, Luc dreamed of going into space, a dream that had become much more vivid since the launch of Sputnik two years earlier. Together, they pondered what it would be like to see Earth from such a distance, to see it rotating slowly before them like a display in a shop window, disclosing its secrets to their eyes alone.

WHEN SHE MENTIONED HER FORMER PROFESSION, THE staff agreed to give her some time with Black Betty, the enormous telescope they had just purchased using one of the largest grants the school had ever received. The head astronomer, a serious-looking woman in her late thirties, stood nervously by as her baby was given over to a stranger. Noting the woman's obvious discomfort, Edna was nonetheless determined to take her time. She kept her eye fixed on that broad circle of sky until it began to populate with meteors. Ten, twenty, thirty abreast: all with identical arcs and extinction points, like waves of soldiers charging an implacable enemy. After a while the pattern seemed to break down. The twinkling of the meteors became staggered, though even in its variability it seemed to follow a prescribed template, like the rotating cylinder of a music box. She imagined each meteor comprising a note in some brooding, extravagant opera.

The intimacy of the telescopic view thrilled her. She could see the chunks of rock in beautiful detail, their alien topography on full display. They were naked before her. *I know you*, she thought absurdly. *I know each of you.* Even beneath the sweeping halos of flame she could see their battered surfaces, distinct like visages, so that they seemed to her to exhibit a quality of volition in their movements. They were tiny saints, smoldering on their martyr's pyre.

When she could no longer tolerate the brightness, she started down the metal staircase again, only to find herself momentarily dazed.

The head astronomer steadied her arm, peering at her cautiously. "Are you all right?" she asked.

Edna regarded her for a moment. The woman's dark hair was fixed with a single bobby pin, the way a child might do it, and there was no hint of makeup on her oval face. She reminded Edna of herself as a young woman. When she had started out in the field, her mentor had told her she needed to tone down her appearance if she wished to be taken seriously as a scientist. "It's better if they don't think of you as a woman at all," he said. Thus, she had eschewed the usual markers of femininity: styled hair, tailored dresses, jewelry. Of course, some women didn't care about such things to begin with, but for her, whose mother had managed to be so glamorous even during the Great Depression, even in secondhand clothes, it had been a sacrifice. Somewhat less nobly, it also allowed her to feel a sense of superiority over the women who chose a more traditional path. They could keep their perfume and their high heels, she thought; she had given herself fully to her work. And yet, after the accident, she'd become one of those women once again. She had relearned how to wear makeup, how to choose the dresses that were best suited for her slender figure, how to curl and arrange her hair so that it was never less than perfectly coiffed. She even walked differently, a sort of slinky, swishing walk that she practiced in the mirror until it became second nature.

Afterward, she'd overheard Everett's friends congratulating him on his good fortune—his homely caterpillar had metamorphosed into a butterfly. But in truth it took some time for him to get used to this new version of her. For months he was awkward and unsure within his own home, clearly missing the plain wife he'd married. Even when she came to him in the evening, baring a shoulder at a time, slipping out of her silky chemise and into his waiting arms, he would avoid her eyes, guiltily, as if he were betraying the woman she used to be. As if *he* were the unfaithful one.

"I'm fine," Edna told the astronomer. "It's just that it seems so dark in here after looking into space."

The woman frowned. "Betty's trained on a fairly dark portion of the sky. You shouldn't be experiencing any visual aftereffects."

Edna produced a noncommittal gesture, waving this off.

"Do you need a ride home?"

"No, no, no. Just the troubles of old age setting in."

The woman seemed to accept this. No one ever questioned the "old age" explanation when it came to eccentric behavior, not even scientists. Edna gave her a quick thank-you and returned home.

As she climbed into bed, she could still see the meteors flashing incandescent behind her eyes. But now the visages they evinced were those of Everett and Luc, their careworn features as clear and sharply wrought as diamonds. What she wouldn't have given at that moment to have either one in bed beside her. For pure animal warmth. For sex. For anything at all, really. The intensity of this impulse came as a shock to her. But then, she was getting so sentimental in her advanced years. Maybe when you had lived beyond a certain age, you started developing quirks of temperament, like Everett's old Plymouth with the phantom rattle.

Luc crossed a line with her, exactly once.

Everett had just left for the night, and Luc, setting aside his newspaper, remarked, "What did you ever see in that man?"

She shook her head and said, firmly, "No."

"What?"

"You don't get to do that."

"Do what?"

"Disrespect him. I love Everett, and I expect you to treat him courteously whether he is present or not."

Luc emitted a little laugh of disbelief. "You can't be serious. How much can you love him when you're in here with me every night?"

"I do. That's all you need to know."

"Then what are we doing here?"

"I don't have to explain myself to you, of all people. I've seen the daily parade of women passing through this room."

"Listen, Edna . . ."

"No, you listen. If you ever say another word against Everett, then this (she encompassed the room in a wide gesture) . . . whatever this is . . . is finished."

"Okay," he agreed at last, taken aback by her vehemence. "Okay, you're right. What the hell do I know about marriage? I'm sorry."

She glared at him a while longer, then nodded, easing down on the bed beside him. For ages they lay in twinned silence, the little seawall formed by their bodies falling fast beneath an encroaching tide of sound. Phones rang. Nurses barked orders at one another. The furnace sputtered on, then off, then on again. Carts rattled down hallways toward God knows where. Custodians with utility brooms whispered past, ridding the corners of their twilight webs. It was as if they were hearing all of these noises for the first time. Edna vaguely recalled a line from a poem Everett had once read to her, something about being awakened by human voices, but the exact words eluded her.

"I am sorry," Luc said again. "I shouldn't have presumed to know your feelings about him. All the married ladies I've been with have hated their husbands."

She laughed, curling in toward him again.

"So where does that leave me?" he asked.

"Well I love you, too, if that makes you feel any better."

"It does."

He touched his hand to her cheek, tracing the crescent of sutures that half-ringed her ear. They had thought she might lose the ear when they first brought her in, but, true to form, she had stubbornly held onto it. "Look, about those other women . . ."

She shook her head. "It doesn't matter."

"You have to know I don't want them."

"I shouldn't have brought it up. Life is complicated, that's all."

"But that's just it. It's not complicated anymore. Not for me."

THEY ARE HERE FOR ME.

The thought was a persistent melody, haunting her hours.

By now, the number of meteors had risen to 340,282, 366,920,936,000,000,000,000,000,000,000,000. (The figure on the computer was almost unthinkable—but then that was mathematics for you, always ready to deliver a quick sock in the gut.) The meteors were no longer visible as separate entities. Instead, her eye could perceive them only as wide, glowing bands—each one distended like a harvest moon—that bent into arcs and interwove themselves in a sweeping tapestry of light. The phenomenon now obscured three-quarters of the sky. Only a small area in the east remained unaffected, like a final window left open, an escape hatch into deep space. And the display was no longer a mute one. Every so often the fanfare was accompanied by a faraway crash, a faint but distinct echo of impact, followed some seconds later by the unmistakable sonic boom. The missiles were beginning to penetrate the atmosphere.

One of the closer ones caused a minor tremor in the ground around her, throwing her briefly off balance. As she steadied herself against a porch beam, there was a moment of intense fear, followed by what could best be described as scientific exhilaration at the thought of recovering and examining one of the meteorites. If she could get one of them under the microscope she could determine the composition. Maybe even make an educated guess as to its provenance. She had the base knowledge for that, at least, and if her expertise came up short there was always the Internet.

When she turned to survey the yard for prospects, she noted that the neighbors several houses down were having a winter barbecue. The husband was outside in his plaid hunting jacket, wielding a spatula and tilting his head in rapid cadence as he sang to himself. Unsurprisingly, he was wholly oblivious to the surrounding tumult, though it seemed to Edna that under the circumstances there was no way he could remain standing, let alone placidly turning steaks on a grill. She wanted to call out to him, to warn him somehow. But of course there was nothing to say. *Howdy, neighbor! How's the wife and kids? Have you noticed that the town is under siege by meteors?*

Bracing for the inevitable sonic boom, her attention was drawn to another fire, this time emanating from the campanile at the top of the hill on campus. Somehow it must have ignited when the meteor hit. It couldn't have been from the object itself—meteors only burned while they were burrowing through the atmosphere, not when they hit the ground. Still, something explosive had happened. Flames glowed in the bell tower windows and crept tendril-like up the sides of the structure. Smoke issued forth in great columns. And though she might have imagined it, she thought she could hear the occasional clang of a bell as the charred framework released it from its fixture. Soon the campanile was completely engulfed: a pitch-dark obelisk within a carapace of fire. She watched it blaze upward like a beacon, as if in welcome to the falling embers of the sky. And the embers answered back, in colors that Edna could now discern with greater clarity than ever before. White, yes, but also pulses of red, yellow, and a bit of airy blue. Although lovely beyond measure, she could not bear it for long. The performance was dizzying, relentless, like one of those laser light shows Everett had dragged her to in the seventies. Her head began to throb. She began to feel disoriented, out of breath. She was aware that she was reeling on the porch steps, her hands grappling for the security of the beam, and then the boom hit, and she was lost in a sea of darkness.

THE DAY OF HER DISCHARGE, SHE WAS SHAKEN TO consciousness by the night nurse at the end of her shift. The sky was just beginning to grow light, and the room was tinted an ethereal blue. Edna was still folded tight against Luc, her head on his chest, his arm curved like an extra rib across her heart.

"Come on," the nurse ordered. "Back to your bed."

Edna, breaking out of her cocoon, sat up groggily and stood to follow her. The floor was cold, and when she turned back to her lover's sleeping form, solitary now, yet still pocketed with their combined warmth, she felt a sharp pang of regret.

"The others thought we should leave you like this, but I argued otherwise."

"Thank you."

The nurse shot her a look of disgust. "I'm not doing this for *you*. I just don't think your husband should have to find out this way."

Later, as Edna stood with suitcase in hand, staring at her rumpled hospital bed, she could hardly believe that it would be for the last time. Already, she felt like an alien. She was wearing the blue shirtdress Everett had brought from home—his favorite, with the tricky top button—but now it just hung off of her body, loose and strange. Her leg ached dully. So did her midsection and the area around her ear. The agonizing pain of the first week was long gone, and yet it had left behind these indelible traces, vibrating like copper filaments in an expanse of soil. And that was just fine with her. She did not want her flesh to forget.

In a few minutes, Everett would be up to fetch her. Take her back to her life. Never mind that she no longer knew where that should be.

She was startled out of her reverie by a voice. "Stay," it said.

She turned to see Luc framed in the doorway, just as he had been the first night he'd come to her. His hair was freshly combed, and his suit jacket was draped rakishly around his still-bandaged torso.

"Marry me," he said. "There are a million research

jobs in New York, especially in the medical field. You could work for anyone you wanted."

She managed a small smile as she gathered up her coat and mohair scarf. On impulse, she draped the latter around his neck before turning away again. "Can't. Someone's got to keep the grasshoppers out of the cornbread."

But then he came up beside her, pulling her in so that he could cradle her neck with his good hand, his thumb coming to rest just behind her mended earlobe. Her breath caught in her throat. The sensation of his fingers on her skin brought back the night's activities with such intensity that she found herself blushing furiously. Had they really done those things? In these antiseptic rooms netted with white? His gaze remained fixed on her, holding her in the moment. "Marry me," he repeated. "Please, Edna. It's possible I could live without you, but I sure as hell don't want to try."

She felt herself yielding to it, her will dissolving before the behemoth of sensate longing. Yes, of course she could do it. She could stay. She and Everett had only been married a few years, after all. He would get over her. He would find someone less complicated and no doubt be far happier than he'd been with her. In her mind's eye a vision began to take shape, an image that was silvered on its surface, almost mirrorlike, and so chimerical it would disappear if held at a different attitude. She saw the lush refuge of the closed ecosystem she might share with Luc. She saw their bodies rising and falling within it, breathing life into each other's mouths until there was no oxygen left in the world. She couldn't help it then: she leaned in to kiss him.

"Okay," she murmured. "Okay, I'll stay with you."

It was then that Everett entered the room. And though Edna abruptly broke free, and Luc's hand fell away from her as if it had been burned, he caught the wintry blooms of their faces. He understood the situation at once.

WHEN SHE FINALLY REGAINED CONSCIOUSNESS IT WAS dawn. The psychedelic pageantry had at last come to an end, and there was a fresh dusting of snow on the ground. With her sweater pulled taut across bony shoulders, she stepped around the house and onto the sidewalk, surveying the damage. At least a dozen neighborhood trees had been felled, ancient oaks, their stumps blackened and forked as if by lightning. A curl of smoke still hovered above the campanile, and she could see similar wisps rising all across town, rising like pillars, as if they were the only things left holding up the sky. Perhaps most ominous was the fact that Arthur's Jack Russell terrier, a chronic barker, had gone strangely silent during the night and had not yet emerged to harass the early-morning joggers. At this rate, Edna thought, there was no way the city could last another night. The next swarm of meteorites would be apocalyptic, beyond all comprehension. They would come thundering to earth like the fabled vengeful gods, eyes like dark matter, mouths a burgeoning corona of flame, and with the carelessness of the immortals they would destroy everything in their paths: good, evil, and all that lay between. Perhaps there would be something like music as they barraged the earth, a sort of crude percussion in place of a requiem. And that would be that.

Edna went inside, dressed, and even took the time to fix her hair into an elegant chignon. Sliding in the jeweled bobby pins, she thought of her mother. She pictured the woman as she had looked in those early mornings before school, in her peach-colored nightgown with the flourish of lace at the top, chewing her lip, her fingers moving nimbly as she braided and pinned Edna's waist-length hair. Edna felt her hand began to flutter slightly, and she waited for the tremor to pass. It was hard to imagine missing someone so much, even after all this time. Her father was just a shadowy figure—he had died when she was only two—but her mother had been Edna's entire world. Her mother had taught her, been firm with her, loved her unequivocally. She had set her on a course and then released her, like an object in space, with no assurances that she would ever reach a safe haven, that she wouldn't be drawn into the gravitational field of an orphan planet or smashed by passing debris. How could a mother entrust her child to such a volatile system? Not for the first time,

Edna was glad she'd never had children of her own. She didn't think she could have withstood the loss.

When she had made herself presentable, she drew on her coat and went in search of a meteorite. She went on foot; there was no reason to take the car. She simply chose the closest smoke plume and followed it.

She found what she was looking for in the center of the sidewalk, within a large wreath of broken cement. The meteorite was small, about the size of an avocado, and irregular in shape. Its blackened surface was riddled with shallow depressions, as though it had already been inspected by an overeager child. Slowly, she extended her hand to it. Under normal circumstances, of course, she would have approached a new specimen with great care, beginning with isolation and containment procedures. But what did it matter now if she was exposed to extraterrestrial germs or a bit of radiation? Projectiles from the sky would kill her long before either of those things could.

She'd heard that meteorites were nearly always cold after they hit, but this one was soothingly warm. It was also heavy—much heavier than a rock its size would normally be. It took her several tries to pick it up. But when at last she grasped it, her whole childhood came blossoming to life beneath her deeply veined fingers. There were the late nights studying math and reading with her mother, the big band music on the radio, the war that flashed by on newsreels at the movie theater, the careful giddiness of walking home from the five-and-dime in her best flowered dress, clutching her very first telescope in her hands. And so it was again, although she was old this time, old and slow, with hair that was silver instead of gold, like an alchemical process in reverse. Once again she was journeying home with an unthinkable treasure clasped firmly to her chest, held there like a lover, as if some force might sense the depths of her yearning and whisk it away from her.

She had almost reached the house when the meteors began again. She could hardly believe it. The sun had only just cleared the horizon, and yet there they were, pearly white missiles against a brightening blue sky. She would have to act quickly if she wanted to examine her find. The neighbor girls were playing in the snow (how much they looked like Luc's daughters, Isabelle and Agnès), and with her rejuvenated eyes Edna could see every streak that ignited the mesosphere behind them, like sparks thrown by an invisible forge. Soon the streaks would begin to overlap, and then would come the familiar pulsating tapestry. After that, who knew? *There are already so many*, she thought as she stepped onto her porch. Where could they all be landing? No doubt they were battering silos and empty cornfields, crashing through farmhouse windows, filling up nearby lakes with their alien rock and metal. It would only be a matter of hours, maybe less, before they overtook the town.

She glared up at the impatient sky. "Wait," she commanded.

Once inside, she quickly set up her microscope on the kitchen table and placed the meteorite down beside it. She didn't know where Everett had kept his sandpaper; instead, she grabbed a pumice stone from the bathroom and sanded down one small section of the surface, just enough to glimpse what lay beneath the sooty crust. It was a much lighter shade inside, as expected, and the interior was filled with what looked like varicolored rice grains. A quick Internet search reminded her of the word for these: *chondrules*. Remnants from the solar nebula, these tiny molten droplets had crystallized into their current configuration long before the solar system even existed, before the sun formed and the planets came ghosting together into bright globes. She swept her fingers lightly across them. *I am touching the very beginning of things, here at the end.*

She was forced to suspend her study of the meteorite as more of its kindred went whistling into structures nearby, setting off car alarms and shattering glass with their time-delayed sonic booms. Through the picture window she watched them fall like a sparse rain. They arrived at odd angles, black and still somewhat scintillant, lobbed like bombs in a children's cartoon. Before long, the house across the street exploded into kindling. It seemed to happen in slow motion: boards flying apart, nails like discharged torpedoes, months of careful carpentry undone in a moment of shocking violence. Edna thought obscurely of the bombing of London, the aftermath of which Everett had seen firsthand. It couldn't have been so different from this.

With great haste, she retrieved a hammer from beneath the kitchen sink, delivering a sharp whack to the larger end of the meteorite. It fractured beautifully, almost unbelievably, into two perfect halves, which curved into her waiting palms like a pair of bird's nests. Only one thin sliver came loose from the center, and it was this fragment that she placed beneath the lens of her microscope.

Just then the house began to shake mightily. She watched, fascinated, as the walls began to expand and contract around her, watched the antique silver knob on the basement door rattle and spin as if it were shifting out of time, blurring like a smile in an old photograph. When it had subsided, she bent over the microscope again. Adjusting the focus, she could more clearly see the olivine and pyroxene that made up the chondrules. She marveled at their glassy metallic sheen, which somehow evoked both Gustav Klimt and the integuments of tropical beetles. Next, she increased the magnification so that only a single grain was visible. Yes, here it was—a missive from the early solar system. Here was the story of all existence, writ small and pitiless, yet suffused with such beauty that she nearly wept looking at it. She could have studied the thing forever, absorbing every lamella, every contour, giving herself over to its faint primordial murmurs.

But forever was rapidly approaching. The whistling and the thunderclaps were nearly constant now. The floorboards began to emit a low hum. Light fixtures swayed, and picture frames were beginning to slide off the walls, shattering as they hit the ground. *This is all happening too fast. But isn't that always the way? There can never be enough time.* She considered the objects around her. A quilt her mother had sewed for her that suggested the branching form of a dendritic cell. Plaques and artifacts from her and Everett's various professional awards. The crescent-shaped table she had crafted during her woodworking phase. Her husband's detailed painting of a pair of lungs, like kite balloons moored against the latest aerial attack. His recliner, too, now quaking, which she had left in its place beside the bookshelf, within easy reach of the French naturalists. And the letter from New York that still lay open on the sideboard. The letter.

IT WAS A DIFFICULT FLIGHT BACK HOME. HARSH words were exchanged over bitter airplane coffee and breakfast pastries. Apologies were made and retracted. Ultimatums were levied. At one point a bizarre game of Truth or Dare ensued, in which Edna answered, with brutal honesty, all the questions put to her concerning her stay in the hospital. Between rebukes they fell to making tender declarations and engaged in outbursts of impassioned kissing. The flight attendants were so bewildered by the couple's vacillations that they ushered them back to the minilounge for the remainder of the flight so as to avoid further scandalizing the passengers. By the time Edna and Everett disembarked, they were not speaking at all. She was contrite, yet indignant. He had settled into a cool detachment and was determined to remain that way. And yet, a month later there they all were, back in New York, hashing out the details of the arrangement between glasses of Bordeaux wine. Luc had brought his French sensibilities to bear in outlining a solution, and Everett, with his ingrained Midwestern pragmatism, having truly inquired of himself what sort of man he was and what he wished to glean from the world, found that he did not object.

It had not been easy, especially at first, when misunderstandings and jealousy nearly wrecked the whole endeavor, but they were all practical, determined people, and they had made it work. As two of the three of them were scientists, they naturally resorted to the scientific method to determine the fairest course of action. They formed hypotheses, conducted experiments, analyzed the results, and applied what they had learned to the next hypothesis. After a few years Luc married Antonia, and the terms of the agreement had to be renegotiated. More than once, the fragile quadrangle came close to shattering under its own precarious weight. There were times when they simply pinballed off one another, every point of contact reverberating in dimensions of pain. Each of them hurt the others; each was hurt in return.

It wasn't until Isabelle and Agnès were born that they were all able to breathe a bit more freely. This was the variable, it seemed, that could at last bring the group into balance. Everett, who had always wanted children, took great joy in ferrying the girls around as if they were his own offspring. He even learned some French so that when he drove them to summer camp or took them on vacations to the Flint Hills, they could continue to use the charming mishmash of English and French they were accustomed to using at home. As Edna could not have children herself, this was something that she was pleased to be able to give her husband. She and Luc, meanwhile, settled on a yearly monthlong trip to Argentina, during which the girls stayed in Kansas with Everett. And Antonia grew ever more confident operating the business in her husband's absence. She had a keen mind for figures and understood intuitively that much of the business of banking boiled down to a strategic display of swagger. She was more than up to the task.

"One day she will take over for good," Luc announced during one of the early handoffs, his face glowing with pride. "The imbeciles will never know what hit them!"

"It's true," Antonia replied with a laugh. "I'm much better at it than you are."

Years passed, and for the bulk of that time Edna

and Everett went about their pleasant lives, attending parties, publishing papers, going to movies and sometimes to Cape Canaveral. They laughed with great frequency. They made love several times a week. They occasionally fought about theories related to their work. It was enough. Every so often she had lapses—they all did—and then the cycle of bruising and mending would begin anew.

She had not chosen the path of least resistance; that was certain. But what else could she have done? She had loved them both. In truth, she had felt herself split in two since the accident. She had walked parallel roads, never existing fully in one world or the other. Until now. Somewhere beneath the pile of newspapers on the sideboard was an apologetic letter from Antonia, dated several weeks back, informing her that her lover had died of advanced liver cancer. He must have known the severity of his condition when he made his last call to her, when he had asked her, with more fatigue than bitterness, "Ah Edna, when did we become old?"

And just like that he was gone—vanished overnight, like poor Everett. Edna had become a single line again, the jagged stroke of a scar upon a leg.

As the house convulsed around her, Edna thought about climbing beneath the heavy dining room table and trying to ride out the wave of destruction. But rationality prevailed; evasive maneuvers at this point would only prolong the inevitable. Instead, she grabbed the pieces of meteorite and hurried to the back porch.

Outside, it really was the end of the world. Meteors the size of cannonballs rained down, crashing like blackened angels into the snow, into the cloistered sanctum of houses, dormitories, cars. Here and there she could see larger ones demolishing entire buildings with a single blow. She chose her final resting place— the Adirondack chair—and pulled Everett's sweater tight around her. Even with the city falling to flame around her she was cold. She yearned for a cup of tea, but it was far too late for that, and so she simply settled back, cradling the meteorite like a child to her breast, the twin sections pressed together like two halves of a heart. Before long the stone grew warmer beneath her fingers. It developed a pulse. It effloresced with energy. It rearranged molecules, displacing both fibers and flesh. She was only mildly surprised when it began to sink into her belly like a brick into soft earth, her transubstantiated skin opening to a portal. Once absorbed, it nestled there, seedlike, unfurling luxuriant sprouts within the grotto of her rib cage, soothing her with its heat, its captured memory of stars. She wondered: was there one such artifact for every person on the planet? Within this endless sea of meteors, could there be a lump of rock and metal aligned to each individual's plenary self—love for love, atom for atom?

All at once a wash of white swept across the sky, starting in the west and moving east. The entire span was disappearing beneath a blanket of meteors. The nearest ones were still visible as brown, still separate, but behind them there was only the white crush of incandescence, dazzling in its intensity. Auras began to attach themselves to nearby objects, just as they did when she had cataracts. But of course there was no procedure that could repair this defect. Edna could only watch as the pearly opacity knit itself together across the firmament, closing like a lid over the civilization beneath it.

Somewhere at the bottom of the world, a mohair scarf flapped in the frozen dark, a sentimental tribute left decades ago. For how long? Soon that token, too, would be destroyed. Loosed from its post by a shell from the sky, it would be buoyed by the wind a final time, curling into something resembling a letter, a hidden sigil, then cut to ribbons or perhaps burned. What did it matter in the end that she had loved and suffered, that she had lost her mother and her husband and her lover, that she had never made a major breakthrough or been awarded a Nobel Prize for her research? What did it matter that she had once dug her toes into the soil at night, or that her body had somehow grown old, becoming this foreign husk that floated free of her bones? She was one among billions, a single mote within a vast sea of matter. There was no great meaning to any of it. Human life was just an engine contrived to move itself forward, individual components notwithstanding.

And yet. There were her meteors, these cherished

markers of her childhood, falling like jewels from a beneficent sky. Like old friends, they had returned to usher in her dissolution. And while they were infinitely varied in shape, size, hue, and trajectory, the light they produced was identical—brilliant, and too brief. It was the same light that even now was beginning to emanate, sunlike, from her chest. Her sinews could no longer contain it. Beneath the black and tan threads of her sweater, her forearms gleamed. Her patellae shone like bright inverted plates. She grew so radiant that the porch balusters began to cast long shadows across the snowy ground. Soon she and her environment would equalize. Light from within would rival that from without, ebbing and flowing like water, tentatively intermingling until at last a stalemate of luminosity would be achieved. *At least my death will be memorable*, she thought. *Assuming there is anyone left to remember it.*

At the end she thought of Everett, with his medical sketches, the MoMA stickers on his microscope, his world-weary grin. And she thought of Luc, with his brawny arm fastened around her in the wreckage, blood weeping from the gash above his eye as he told her that everything was going to be all right, all right.

She smiled.

And like the dinosaur she was, waited calmly for extinction.

AUTHOR'S
ACKNOWLEDGMENTS

Deep and abiding thanks go to:

My publishers, Mary Ann Rivers and Ruthie Knox at Brain Mill Press, for their tireless work, passion, and loving attention to detail in making this book a reality. You are truly the best.

Sam Battersby and Ann O'Connell, who created the incomparable art for this book, and Ranita Haanen for the spectacular cover design.

My parents, for absolutely everything. I love you!

My wonderful husband, Nick, who has believed in me from the beginning, and who has had to endure countless conversations about what fictional people would or wouldn't do in a given situation. Please don't turn into a merman.

My brilliant and beautiful daughter, Zooey, who transforms the world for me every day.

My aunt Judy, who started me reading speculative fiction at a young age.

My very cool in-laws, Janelle and Joe, for always asking what I'm working on.

Mrs. Conner, my fourth-grade teacher, who taught me to love science (and learning).

My many friends who have served as readers and

encouraged me through the years as I wrote wacky words about wacky subjects that often baffled them. Thomas and Laurie, Susan and Paul, Mike and Lisa, and more recently, Jess, Brita, Rachael, Martha, and Emily.

The people who maintain the Hollywood Forever Cemetery, where I found Valentino's final resting place and, not incidentally, the inspiration for "A Kiss for a Dead Film Star."

The wonderful band Trailer Bride, whose creepy song "The Ghost of Mae West" nearly got me pregnant.

Gabriel Garcia Marquez, for making the impossible possible.

Coffee, for existing.

ABOUT THE AUTHOR

Photograph courtesy Chelsea Donoho

Karen M. Vaughn rattled around eastern Kansas for much of her life before finally settling in Lawrence, where the best weirdos are. For several years she edited for a medical journal (just ask her about the famous Eyeball Issue), and now does academic editing on a freelance basis. She loves reading and writing off-kilter fiction. Her work has appeared in *A cappella Zoo, Whiskey Island Magazine, Illya's Honey,* and *REAL: Regarding Arts & Letters.* Karen enjoys traveling to mountainous places with her husband and daughter, watching supernatural horror films, and teaching herself guitar so that she can fill in for Jack White if he should ever become ill.

CREDITS

AUTHOR	Karen M. Vaughn
EDITOR	Mary Ann Rivers
COPYEDITOR	Ruthie Knox
PROOFREADER	Annamarie Bellegante
COVER ILLUSTRATION	Samantha Battersby
COVER DESIGN	Ranita Haanen
INTERIOR ART	Ann O'Connell
INTERIOR DESIGN	Williams Writing, Editing & Design

BRAIN MILL PRESS WOULD LIKE TO ACKNOWLEDGE
the support of the following patrons:

Noelle Adams

Rhyll Biest

Katherine Bodsworth

Lea Franczak

Barry and Barbara Homrighaus

Kelly Lauer

Susan Lee

Sherri Marx

Aisling Murphy

Audra North

Molly O'Keefe

Virginia Parker

Cherri Porter

Erin Rathjen

Robin Drouin Tuch

Made in the USA
Charleston, SC
16 August 2016